BAD REPUTATIONS

THE BREAKING THROUGH SERIES BOOK 1

BARBARA DELEO

FOREWORD

This title was previously published, in part, as Dishing up Desire.

PROLOGUE

*a*nd now I'd like you to take a moment to centre yourself, look deep within your most secret places to determine the barriers that you're unconsciously putting in your way to success in life."

Bah . . . loney!

Kirin Hart yanked out the ear pods that still carried the softly irritating voice of Sapphire Green - *Whole Life Coach* - and skated them across her desk. Surely she wasn't the only one in this online coaching session to have aching molars every time Sapphire asked them to "dig beneath your fragile facade" and "stop stroking your immature ego."

Kirin blew away her bangs with a hot breath and leaned back in her chair. She scanned the names of the twenty-four other people on this call. Were they women? Men? Business people? Students?

Sapphire had insisted everyone would be completely anonymous, so people had some wildly made-up names. There was "BlueWolverine" who was trying to learn how to be assertive with their mother-in-law; "Lucy Lu" who was

I

trying to decide if they should change careers; and Kirin's favorite "Bottomless Brenda" who was having some complex family issues she wanted to address once and for all.

Kirin clicked on the icon next to Brenda's name and a separate chat window popped up.

Kirin: *How's your flimsy facade looking, Brenda?*

A notification popped up that indicated Bottomless Brenda was typing.

Bottomless Brenda: *My immature ego's gone off sulking in the corner to eat Ben and Jerry's Salted Caramel. If yours wants to play hooky maybe we can hang for a while.*
Kirin: *Here voluntarily or dragged kicking and screaming?*
Bottomless Brenda: *Kinda voluntarily. As I said in my intro I've got some family stuff going on and wanted to get a handle on how to tackle it. Didn't want to be doing that face-to-face in a small town.*
Kirin: *Your real name Bottomless Brenda?*
Bottomless Brenda: *No, and believe me I've got plenty of bottom. I make store mannequins, so I'm often surrounded by headless torsos. Men from the waist up. My name's Gwin.*

Men from the waist up. Wouldn't that solve a whole lot of my problems, Kirin thought.

Kirin: *Cool name, Gwin. Short for something?*
Gwin: *Guinevere, as in King Arthur and stuff.* 😊 *My mom's Avalon too so it's all my Nan's fault. What brings you to Sapphire's den. Are you here because of your name?*

Kirin's eyes darted to the name she'd given herself. Surely Gwin hadn't worked out who she was? She'd been super careful not to reference her job or anything that might identify her. "Broken Hearted." *Broken Hart.* That just about summed her up.

Kirin: *Not at all. Just a silly play on words. It's more the way I feel every night at 8pm when we have to go online.*
Gwin: *Kiwi6 is a bit of a laugh. That story she told the first day about being traumatized by a rabbit made of jello made me wet my pants a little bit.*
Kirin: *Let's ask if she wants to play hooky, too.*
Gwin: *Yes!*

Kirin clicked on *Add to Chat* and typed in *Kiwi6.* "Want to hang out?" she typed. "Promise it's a jello rabbit free zone."

Kiwi6: *Hey Brenda and Broken Hearted. Nice to meet you. I was trying to dig deep but couldn't get past the custard donut I had about half an hour ago.*
Kirin: *Just call me, K. And this is Gwin.*
Gwin: *I'm guessing you're from New Zealand, Kiwi?*
Kiwi6: *I'm Ellie and yes I'm in New Zealand right now. You guys?*
Gwin: *Brentwood Bay, Northern California. Born, raised and still chained to the place unfortunately . You, K?*

"San Francisco," Kirin typed, enjoying the fact she could be anonymous. Someone from New Zealand wouldn't know who she was, but someone from California possibly would.

.   .   .

Gwin: *I guess that's the beauty of the online world. We can all be anyone from anywhere. Kinda levels the playing field.*
        Doesn't it.

Ellie: *It's kinda not what I imagined, this course. I thought we'd get more practical ways to organize our lives, set goals, that sort of thing. I spend the hour feeling pretty stink about myself and then spend the next day worrying that I haven't done all the homework she's set.*
Gwin: *Oh, I HEAR you!*
Kirin: *What made you take the course?*
Ellie: *I'm back home in New Zealand to do a community project and it's kinda delicate so I wanted to give myself a few assertiveness skills.*
Kirin: *I've always wanted to go to New Zealand.*
Ellie: *Spent most of the last few years in the States which is where I heard about Sapphire. It's lovely to be home.*
Gwin: *A community project sounds fun. What sort?*
Ellie: *It's quite a big thing. I need to get the whole town on board so I was hoping this might give me some inspiration for how to stay strong.*
Gwin: *Thinking you'll have some resistance?*
Ellie: *Yes resistance, and some ghosts that I'm going to have to revisit . . .*
Kirin: *Kinda like a high school reunion. When you know you really shouldn't care about what everyone will think of you but some deep, sick part of yourself is desperate for them to see you as accomplished and cool now.*
Ellie: *Exactly. And you K? Why did you sign up?*
Kirin: *I didn't want to. It's a condition of my probation.*

There was a distinct pause in messaging.

Kirin: *Oh, not THAT kind of probation!!!! I've been told I need an image makeover. I'm on a kind of behavior probation...*

Gwin: *What the ACTUAL! Please don't tell me it's a guy who's told you that!!*

Kirin: *It's a few guys and a couple of women. They're on my company board and apparently my image is bringing down the brand so they want to give me a zjuszh up – (don't know if that's the way you spell it!)*

Ellie: *Your image as in the way you look? Clearly I can't see you, but I can already tell you're friendly and quick and you're funny. Who cares what you look like?*

Kirin: *Everyone in the business except me apparently. How about you Gwin? Think this course is going to help you with your family stuff?*

Gwin: *I don't know anymore. I'm trying to get my sister and niece to move out of my mom's house and move to the city. Things are a bit wobbly for my niece—she's twelve—and I'd kinda like to see her have different teenage years to me and her mom.*

Ellie: *And your mom doesn't want you to go?*

Gwin: *You've got it. I'm twenty-nine. I don't think it's too unreasonable for me not to want my mom folding my underwear anymore.*

Kirin: *Will your mom have a good support network after you leave?*

Gwin: *She knows the whole town. She's had a hairdressing salon since she was in her twenties and she's got a tight group of girlfriends. I've told her to come to the city with us but she won't even consider it.*

Kirin: *You know I have got one useful thing from this whole course... When she asked us what we're afraid of...*

Ellie: *Yeah, I agree, that was quite helpful. Want to share?*

Kirin: *I guess I'm afraid that if people see that my outside doesn't match my inside they won't believe in me anymore.*
Gwin: *I still don't really understand why you need to change your image so much. How do you think those people see you now?*
Kirin: *That I'm too old fashioned, that I only appeal to a small group of people. They think if they modernize me, I'll expand the brand.*
Ellie: *Any part of you think they could be right?*
Kirin: *Yeah, I get what they mean but I resent the fact that my skills can't speak for themselves. How about you guys? Did you do the fear exercise?*
Gwin: *Yeah, it was pretty easy for me. I'm afraid of my niece having a challenging life like my sister's had. Getting into the same sorts of risky situations. Also not having the same little life her mom and I have both had.*
Kirin: *Little life?*
Gwin: *When people know you—or they think you do. They know your family, your history, that time you had a meltdown in the faucet aisle at Home Depot. Sometimes that's a great thing, but often it can just lead to a whole lot of judgment.*
Ellie: *I just realized, you're about to do the opposite of me. You're breaking away from the life that's defined you for so long and I'm breaking back in.*
Gwin: *And what part of that makes you afraid?*
Ellie: *Having to revisit some tough things that happened to me back there. Face memories that hurt a lot.*
Kirin: *That's a whole lot of pressure to have to face up to. How long will you have to be there?*
Ellie: *A few months. I've done a lot of ground work and now I'm here I'll need to call some town meetings and get the project started. Things could get spiky.*
Gwin: *Anyone special with you for support?*

Ellie: *No. I've been too busy organizing everything to be dating lately. You guys?*

Kirin: *HELL. NO. I was separated and almost divorced when my husband died a few years ago. and I'm completely off dating for the next millennium or so. How about you Gwin? Leaving anyone behind in Brentwood Bay?*

Gwin: *No. I live with my Mom, my sister and my niece, so dating hasn't been easy. My sister will leave a string of broken hearts. Who knows what might happen for me in the big city though?*

Kirin: *You know what, you guys? I've got more out of this chat than I have from every other session put together. Why don't we keep this up?*

Elie: *You mean chat just the three of us instead of listen to Sapphire?*

Kirin: *Yes! Like we're a lifeboat of three, helping each other navigate the next few months together. I can handle maybe one session with Sapphire a week, not the once a day thing she wants us to do for the next month.*

Gwin: *BEST IDEA! I've got amazing girlfriends and really good work mates, but in a small town it's sometimes hard to be completely honest about what you're feeling, you know I'd love to be able to share that stuff with you guys.*

Ellie: *I can understand that. Not wanting anything to get back to your family. LOVE this idea, K. My sister will be here for a bit while I'm working on the project, but she went through the same tough time I did and we've kind of never talked about the really hard stuff, you know?*

Kirin: *Hugs for that. Okay, why don't we say the one big thing we want to achieve this week and then we can cheer lead each other on when we meet back tomorrow.*

Gwin: *Okay. I want to convince my sister that us leaving town is the best thing for the three of us and for us to start putting plans in place. You, Ellie?*

Ellie: *To have the strength to go back to Rata Cove and have some quiet time there by myself before I have to call town meetings. What about you K?*
Kirin: *I want to bite my tongue, see the bigger picture and the greater good for the business. Maybe try not to have the next image consultant quit. Okay, girls, It's a date!!*

*B*lake Matthews stepped from the elevator into the cool basement of Hart Corporation and sucked in a lungful of air. The sweet smell of something toasted and warm assaulted his nose, filled his mouth, and confirmed that Kirin Hart, America's fallen-angel chef, was close by.

Hands slung in his pockets, he strode down the bare concrete corridor toward the enticing smells and cooking sounds, ready to meet the challenge of fixing Mrs. Hart's public image that had been so spectacularly annihilated.

Because she'd broken the last few consultants who'd tried to tackle this mammoth assignment, he'd stepped in to minimize catastrophic fallout to the PR company he was about to buy. The board of directors had given him fourteen days to prove he had what it took to preserve the integrity of their company or they wouldn't sell to him.

He'd turn the situation around in ten.

A photograph from the file his investigator had put together reeled through his mind—the focused woman carefully disguised beneath homely outfits, pastel cardigans, and blond hair in a sweet braid. She'd certainly crafted the look of dependable domestic goddess well. Pity her husband and the other half of *Cooking with Hart* had died mid coitus with a much younger woman, thereby smashing their wholesome image and the public's love for them to smithereens. And that was just the beginning of her problems.

Confidence pumped sweetly through his veins. He'd never failed at a job this big, and didn't intend to start now, especially with the expansion of his business at stake. He'd overhaul Mrs. Hart—beige trouser suit and all—and be back home in New York in no time.

At the end of the corridor, he stopped in an open doorway.

Behind a long stainless-steel counter strewn with cooking paraphernalia, a woman had her back to him as she stirred something on an enormous industrial stove. He leaned a shoulder against the doorjamb, the low roar of overhead fans sucking away steam and allowing him to watch her unnoticed.

A loose blond ponytail, falling from beneath a small black hat, rested between narrow shoulders. His gaze tracked lower to where the strings of a black chef's apron fell down the back of a plain tan skirt hugging a perfectly rounded bottom. He took a step into the room, but still she worked, backward and forward. Her movements were sexily hypnotic—stirring and shuffling implements, occasionally dusting a hand across the curve of her hip—oblivious to the fact he couldn't pull his eyes away.

Still unaware of him, she leaned to the back of the stove, dipped a spoon into one of the pans, and steadying a hand beneath, lifted it to her face and blew. As she opened her mouth and slowly slid the spoon between dusky lips, the secret intimacy of it caused his stomach muscles to clench, and on reflex, he cleared his throat. When she spun around, the spoon clattered to the floor, her moist mouth forming a perfect O.

"Can I help you?" She reached for a cloth to clean up the liquid splattered across the counter and all down her front. "You must be lost."

He took a step into the room. "Not lost. I was looking for you. Don't stop what you're doing, I was enjoying it." He moved forward. "Blake—"

"How did you get in? This is a restricted area." Her eyes flicked to her apron and back at him, the creamy skin at her jaw tightening as she wiped away the mess.

"Through the door." He tried a grin, but she dropped her gaze.

"But I have security."

The chilly reception wasn't surprising. Angela Jenkins, the last consultant on this job, had described Kirin Hart as defensive and suspicious—and that was before Kirin had told her that she didn't need their services any more. "Might want to check on that security." He stepped around a stack of cardboard cartons. "I told your doorman who I was, and he let me come straight down."

Finally, sparking caramel eyes focused on him, and she stopped still. "What can I do for you?"

He pulled up an industrial-looking stool and sat. "If you're not going to continue cooking, best turn the stoves off. This could take a while."

She laid both hands on the counter and hooked him with a "give me orders if you dare" look as her chest rose, then fell. "The expansion might've fallen through, but I still need these new stoves." The mask was edged with hard-nosed determination and was even more of a turn on than watching her cook. Her tongue peeped out and she moistened her lips. "I'll downsize the chillers, though, so you can take the big one in the next room. It was the last one you sent."

She removed her apron. A cream blouse in soft fabric skimmed her breasts and sat lightly across a gently rounded stomach. It had a V-neck but must have had two dozen tiny pearl buttons all down the front and reminded him of a particularly up-tight Sunday school teacher he'd once had.

At her throat, a thin gold chain lay against her milky skin with the letter K in a flourishing script. "We won't be needing the new office furniture you delivered last month, either. You can take that back." She waved a delicate hand, and thin gold bracelets tinkled on her wrist. "I'm sorry but I don't have time to discuss this right now." She turned back to the stove. "Make an appointment with my P.A. and she'll coordinate with you. I'm sure you'll find your way out."

He raised an eyebrow, intrigued by her ball-breaking attitude and the fact they'd had an entire conversation without him saying a word.

If he was a supplier of cooking equipment, or a repo man, he'd be throwing out some pretty choice expletives right now in response to her attitude. Lucky for her, he had a few more manners than she was displaying. No wonder she was such a PR disaster. He shrugged out of his suit jacket and, finding nowhere to put it on the crowded counter, laid it across his knee. "I've come to discuss your contract with Dent and Douglas."

Her shoulders straightened. "My contract with Dent and Douglas is finished. I explained to Angela Jenkins that it wasn't working out." She turned and played with the strings of the apron. "If there are things to sign my lawyer will take care of it."

She leaned closer, and the K slipped beneath the fabric to a part of her he couldn't see.

He swallowed, then refocused. Given her significant business troubles, the fight she still had left inside was admirable, and surprisingly sexy. "I'm Angela's replacement."

Her eyes darted from the apron to his face. "May I see your card?"

Shit. His stomach clenched. He was going to have enough trouble making her come around if she thought he *worked* for Dent and Douglas. If she knew he was D and D's new buyer and that they wouldn't sell until he'd fixed her situation, she'd be the one in the driver's seat, and no way was that happening. His real identity could be saved for later. "I left my last card with your guy upstairs. Call him."

She turned as if looking for her phone, then seemed to think better of it. "In case you haven't quite got the message, I've changed my mind. I don't want an image consultant anymore. Thanks for your time. I'm sorry it was wasted."

Good. She believed him. But he wasn't going anywhere. "No consultant? Why?"

There was that tongue again, slipping between her lips, and he found his eyes being constantly pulled there. "Because I need to get myself out of this mess." A flare of pain blossomed in her eyes.

So, there *was* a heart beating behind that tough shell. "And how do you intend to do that on your own? From what I understand, your brand's looking about as attractive as a high-speed train wreck right now. And you're the one who's still standing on the accelerator. Seems to me like you need a lot of professional help. Fast."

She pulled the hat from her head and tiny blond hairs stood up at different angles. The pain was still in her eyes, and her face had softened. "By working hard, cooking well, things I've done since the start of my career. No amount of PR talk and fancy outfits is going to do that for me."

He picked up some sort of metal cooking utensil and turned the handle. "I'd suggest it wasn't your cooking or your work ethic that got you into this mess so it's not likely they'll get you out. Your brother did the right thing, hiring the best PR firm in town to turn your fortunes around. You'll never put this right on your own. From what I understand, if you don't act soon you're going to have a parade of removal men banging down your door. And they might not be as gentlemanly as me."

She'd rolled the apron into a ball and threw it to the side. "Flynn has a good heart, but he has no clue about this industry." She rubbed her forehead. "Your colleague, Angela, started telling me what I should wear, how I should speak, who I should be associating with." Her eyes flashed as she spoke.

"All excellent advice which I hear you refused to take."

She laid a hand at her throat, her slim fingers stroking the pale skin that looked as silky as the fabric covering the rest of her top half. "What did you say your name was?"

"Matthews." He threw her his 'trust-me' smile. "Blake Matthews."

"Well, thanks, Blake Matthews, but I don't require the services of Dent and Douglas anymore. I'm happy to handle this on my own." She picked up a towel and turned back toward the stove. "If you don't mind, I have a party to cater and you're holding me up." She bent down to look in an oven, then pulled open the door.

"What's the party?"

She leaned in and put a skewer into the cake. When she

drew it back, he noticed her long, dark lashes as she surveyed the end. "It's for the son of a friend."

"Sweet Sixteen? Or twenty-first? You must be glad for the work. I've heard that the catering side of Hart Corp. has taken a big hit." He turned the handle on the cooking thing and a blade inside nearly sliced his finger off.

She shut the oven door hard and turned, skewer pointing toward him, cheeks flushed. "It's Niko's fourth birthday, and unless you want to lose a thumb, I suggest you put that down. There's a reason we don't let the public down here."

The public? Prickles rose on his neck for a second, and then he reminded himself how much he enjoyed the challenge of getting people like Kirin Hart on his side. Two could play at her game.

He nodded slowly and placed the cutting thing gently on the counter. "How long have you been catering birthday parties for pre-schoolers? And is that sort of work going to stop your business imploding? Can't imagine there's a whole lot of profit in Jell-O molds and Funnel cakes, or whatever kids eat at parties these days."

She sighed. "My business is none of *your* business, Mr. Matthews."

"Ah, but that's where you're wrong." He met the challenging spark in her stare and smiled slowly. He'd come from New York to buy Dent and Douglas—the jewel in his crown of image consultancies and PR firms—and suddenly they'd put a halt to the sale. The Hart Corp debacle—and the resulting media circus—was destroying the reputation San Francisco's most famous PR company had worked fifty years to develop. They wanted proof that Blake had the capacity to maintain the integrity of their name. And they wouldn't sell until he'd proven he could fix Kirin Hart and her image.

He put his palms flat on the cool counter top. "I don't do failure, Ms. Hart, and right now Dent and Douglas have a contracted client whose image *hasn't* been changed, whose fortunes *haven't* been turned around as they assured her they would be. Where I come from, we call that a dud rap. I don't do dud raps. In fact, I've never been involved in one, and don't intend to start now."

Kirin tucked a stray piece of hair behind her ear. "Angela spent her whole time suggesting I didn't know how to dress or do my hair. I'm a chef, not a catwalk model. Surely the decision about whether to carry on a contract is up to the client," she said, voice tight.

"That might be the case if that client wasn't the biggest image disaster in American history. The whole world and his PR machine know D and D took you on. Their reputation will be worth nothing if we don't see the contract through."

She took a moment before answering. "And why are you so interested in me? Are you the bad cop, the guy who tries to muscle in and rough up the client when she's not toeing the line?"

He adjusted himself on the stool, hooked by her candor and the way her chest rose in defiance. He hadn't counted on her spitfire responses, or his responses to them. He'd dealt with a lot of people in his career, but no one had captured his fascination as quickly as Kirin Hart. This was a woman who believed in herself and her image so much she was prepared to fight to the death for it. Trouble was, the media was nailing the lid on her career's coffin hour-by-hour and unless something drastic happened, she'd have nothing left. And his plan to add the crowning company in his coast-to-coast empire would be finished.

"I'm no bad cop, and I'm not interested in you, Mrs. Hart. I'm interested in your image. They're two entirely different things. When you begin to understand that, we might start getting somewhere."

For a second, something passed across her face, almost as if she'd been hurt by what he'd said, but then she stood straighter. "I've told you, I'm not interested. I'll pay the contract cancellation fee and be done with it. And please don't call me Mrs. Hart, my name is Kirin."

"You'll renege on the contract and just wait for everything to go up in a smoke of debts? All the things you've worked so hard and so long for?"

The skewer clanged as she dropped it on the countertop. "People have been taking from me since my husband died." Her bottom lip wobbled before she cleared her throat. "In fact, since well before that and right up to the present day. I'm used to it, but I'm not going to let you do it, too."

"You mean your husband's affair? The fact he died when he was with his mistress? Or the sexual harassment accusation against you?"

Blood drained from her face, and her eyes glistened. "You know about all of it?"

He crossed his arms. "The way I understand it, firstly your husband single handedly smashed your career, your livelihood and image, and then a low life decided to kick you while you were down. You want that false accusation to be the way you're remembered? And for everything you worked for before your husband's deception to be worth nothing?"

"It's already happened," she murmured and looked up at him. Her shoulders had slumped, and the defeated look on her face stirred something deep inside. For the shortest second, her cultivated control was replaced with soft vulnerability and a gut wrenching sadness, and the contrast was mesmerizing.

She lifted her chin and whispered, "No. No, I don't want to be remembered that way."

"Then let me help you."

She picked up a knife and sliced it through a stick of butter. "I've been relying on people for too long. Letting other people determine my life's path. It's time I took charge."

He swallowed, his heart throwing in an extra beat for her vulnerability. "I'm the best there is at turning around public images, Kirin. Come back on board and I'll have journalists phoning you for interviews, invitations to talk shows and A-list parties. I can have your image back on track, brighter than you ever thought possible, in no time."

She reached behind her for a small copper pot and put the butter in. "And what makes you so sure you can achieve this magic? Is a superhero outfit lurking under that smart suit?" Her first real smile flitted across her face and it dazzled. "A pair of underpants over the tights underneath? I'm sorry but I don't need rescuing by you or anyone else."

He didn't usually have to spell out his experience. Most people he dealt with had been on a waiting list for his services for months and knew every last detail. "I've been in the image industry for fourteen years. I started work at sixteen as an international model and quickly learned that the way you portray yourself can make, or cost you, millions. The image the public currently has of you, if I may be so blunt, is a woman who's down trodden and beaten." He waited until she looked directly at him. "I can already tell that's not the real you at all."

She was quiet for a moment, then shook her head. "Thanks for your interest, but I'm going to do this on my own. Now, if you don't mind, I have a hundred cupcakes to frost."

Blake reached into his pocket, pulled out his phone, and swiped to the picture he wanted before sliding it across the counter to her. "How's this 'doing it on your own' working out for you?"

She looked down at the picture on the screen, and a flush swept up her neck. "Yeah, not one of my finest moments."

"You flipped the bird at twenty-five photographers and the image spread across nationwide news channels and is viral on Tik Tok. If this is part of your strategy to go it alone, can I quietly suggest you're making a dog's breakfast of it? My research tells me you've been hounded by photographers for weeks, that you even had to have one removed from your front yard; all reasons to be upset, but the middle finger salute doesn't quite fit with your current image."

She swept her tongue across her lip again, and in an unbidden flash, his pulse spiked. He suffocated the rogue reaction and focused.

"How much do you know about cooking, Mr. Matthews, and how much about my career?"

"It's Blake," he said. "I know that you and your husband started young and built a multi-million dollar business. People saw your shows, bought your cookbooks, your grocery products, the whole, 'Cooking with Hart' brand as defining integrity, reflecting traditional values and wholesome living. I also know that your husband cheated on you with a much younger woman for years and made a lie of the down home and dependable brand you'd both so carefully created."

Kirin had switched off the stoves and fans and leaned against the counter. A connection was growing. "And the rest of it?"

Blake cleared his throat. "I know that on the back of your husband's death, a disgruntled employee saw his chance to get a big payout and said you sexually harassed him. All my sources say it's a nasty, vindictive lie—a complete fabrication but when your board insisted you settle out of court, it made people thought if there's smoke, there's fire."

"I didn't. . . I would never. . ." She shook her head, her eyes luminous. "Even the thought that I could use my position to do that to someone is *so* abhorrent." Her voice wobbled on the last few words, and he wondered for a second if she might cry, but she stood straighter. She was motionless. "Do you believe that's really what I'm like?"

He shrugged and pinned his gaze to hers. "What I believe is irrelevant. What the public currently sees is a woman who's still trying to present an image of traditional values and buttoned down control. A woman who's become an enigma—someone they don't really know anymore, and it's taken the focus right away from what you're best at— your cooking business. Not only will all that go away if you agree to my plan, but we can harness that new image of you to build a whole new brand."

"And what would your strategy be? To tell me to change the way I dress, the way I speak, like Angela did?"

"There would be some of that," he admitted. "And a few lessons in what *not* to say."

She reached across to a pile of linen and pulled out a fresh apron and hat. "Thank you for your time, Mr. Matthews. I appreciate your interest and concern, but part of what's wrong in my life is that I've put too much of my trust in people—especially pushy men—who've only wanted to use me for their own gains. You're not going to be another of those people, so I thank you for your time. Please close the door behind you." And with that, she turned her back and walked away.

2

Three days later Kirin burst through the double glass doors of the TV station, did a swift sidestep towards a bunch of schoolgirls huddled at a bus stop, then took a quick right to where she'd left her car parked in a side alley.

Slinging her shoulder bag further onto her back she started to run, the clump, clump of her dark brown lace-ups echoing the thump of her heart. The embarrassment—no, the body-aching, mind-numbing *shame* of the television interview she'd just endured, was enough to make her want to throw up here and now.

They'd sold the interview to her as an opportunity to start fresh with the public, to explain the pressure she'd been under, talk about the bad choices she'd made, but instead they'd told her about some sort of sex tape they had exclusive access to. And in that horrifying moment she'd ripped the microphone from her blouse, stumbled over a camera cable, and run from the building.

If she wasn't so angry, she might cry the hot, hard tears that stung behind her nose. But she *was* angry. Blood-boiling, head-spinning angry. Waking up every day in this nightmare wouldn't be so bad if there was some chance of things getting better, but she could see the bottom of the hole she'd fallen into rushing towards her and it was going to hurt like hell when she hit it. Tears clouded her vision and for the first time in weeks, she didn't try to hold them back.

As she got closer to her car, the fear of what might be chasing her was overshadowed by the sight of someone lounging on her hood.

Blake Matthews.

The man who'd been hijacking her thoughts since she'd asked him to leave her kitchen a few days ago was here in perfect profile and looking like he owned the road. He was so ruggedly self assured, so effortlessly unforgettable, and his all-male perfection was not what she needed right now. Hurriedly, she blinked away the tears.

Casting a look over her shoulder and seeing only two photographers and a reporter in high heels making a dash toward her, she made a final push to the car.

"Need to get away!" she called, as Blake eased himself from the car and strolled to the driver's door.

Hand casually slung in a pocket, he tipped his sunglasses up. "Keys. Give them to me."

"No! What—?"

"They're coming after you." His intense gaze didn't move from her face. "And you're in no state to drive. Keys."

"Kirin, Kirin!" a reporter with an English accent shouted. "What about the sex-tape? What sort of things can we expect to see on it? The full monty or just a bit of slap and tickle?"

She crumpled against the side of the car.

"Keys. Now."

Mindless, she tossed them in his direction and as soon

as he had the door unlocked, threw herself into the passenger seat. In a second he'd gunned the engine and they were shooting down the alley toward the main road.

"That was like a bad movie," she finally managed, as she rearranged her skirt and blouse and fought to regain her breath.

"You mean a good movie." Blake's broad hands gripped her steering wheel, the bright white of his shirt cuff contrasting with the warm tan of his fingers. For a minute she had to think twice about what he'd just said.

"How in all hell could my life resemble a good movie?"

Sleek designer shades covered his eyes, but the quirk at his mouth suggested he was teasing. "In the *bad* movies, the girl runs screaming from the building and is either knocked down by a Number Ten bus, or the buff guy waiting at her car turns out to be the exact same one she's been trying to get away from." He flicked the turn signal and Kirin sat mesmerized by the tiny dimple in his cheek each time he smiled, and the perfectly crafted stubble she'd only seen on movie stars. "In the *good* movies the guy waiting at the car's the hero, the one who's going to solve the problem she was running from."

She reached down into her bag and switched off her phone to stop it from buzzing constantly. Her pulse slowed. "And the woman can't just get into her car and remove herself from the problem on her own no matter which situation she's in, right? She'll always need a man."

He turned the wheel, and they swung around a corner. "Hell, no. I wouldn't pay to see a movie like that. No fun at all." He grinned, all mischief and suggestion. "Unless there was a sex tape in it."

She dropped her head and the same hot horror from five

minutes ago came surging back, but this time it didn't hurt quite so bad. Blake's smile was still warming her.

He took a quick look in the rearview mirror and, seemingly satisfied, finally turned toward her. "So, is there a sex tape?"

"A tape? No, of course there isn't! He was an *employee*. I would never, *ever* have let myself get into a compromising position with him. It's possible he taped a conversation and edited it to suggest something else. . . But nothing physical happened between Trent and me. Ever."

She chewed the inside of her lip, the old swirl of panic taking hold again. "Knowing what he's capable of, he could've engineered the whole thing to look like something else, though. There's all that deep fake stuff where they manipulate videos of people to make it look as though they're saying outrageous things. Do you think that's what he's done?"

Blake blew air through his teeth. The strong, confident profile she'd spent the last three days trying to forget about was even more mesmerizing without a counter top between them. Rugged jaw, a smile that split his face, and white teeth that dazzled—it was screamingly obvious why he'd been an international model. Those sorts of looks were one in a million. She'd never met a man—anyone—as naturally stunning, and she couldn't stop looking at him. "I have a god daughter who was harassed by a boy in high school and while my first instinct was to take him out, the best way I could help her was by giving her tools to help herself. I can offer you the same. They didn't play any of the tape on 'The Williams Show,' did they?"

"I didn't give them a chance. As soon as he started to ask me about it I panicked and ran." Without thinking, she clutched his arm. "Oh, God, you don't think they'd have played it after I left? When I settled with Trent it was under the strict condition neither of us would speak about what had happened or the agreement we came to, so why is this coming up now?"

He glanced down to where her fingers lay on his forearm and smiled. She drew back with a start, the memory of his warm, hard body imprinted on her fingertips.

"It's not Bray talking about it, that's why." He looked out the windshield again. "He's leaked this so it can be kept in the public eye longer. Destroy your reputation even further. He sure as hell has a vendetta against you."

"That's because he didn't get the position he was after in my company." She blew out a long breath, strangely calmed by Blake's soothing voice and his commanding presence beside her. "I'm guessing it's not a coincidence that you were leaning against my car. That you knew I was at the taping. And, by the way, where are we going?"

"I found out from a contact that you were doing the Larry Williams show and guessed the result. Larry's ratings haven't been that great lately, and he's in for the shock factor. If you'd asked me. . ." He paused for effect. "Which you didn't because you don't have an image consultant anymore, I'd have told you to stay well clear of him. And I'm taking you home. Right now you need to feel safe."

Tears threatened again at his caring tone, but she placed her palms together and squeezed them between her knees, trying to keep it together. She was so out of her depth it felt like she was drowning, watching everything she'd worked so hard and long for disappear into the mist. "You think I'm naïve, don't you?"

They stopped at a traffic light and he lifted his glasses onto his head, turning his full attention to her. "Naive? No. You're a chef and a businesswoman who doesn't have the required skill set to combat the likes of Larry Williams or Trent Bray. It's nothing to be ashamed of, but there's plenty you can do about it."

The soft, enquiring look in his eyes sent heat rushing to her cheeks. It had been such a long time since anyone had said something so caring to her, and even though he was only doing it to get her to re-sign with him, it sent a warm clutch to her chest. "You really think so?"

He moved with the traffic, and she was relieved to not be under his bone-melting stare any longer. "Look, Kirin, I wouldn't know a squash from a sweet potato and couldn't care if I ever did. Food holds no interest for me whatsoever. But if my life and my reputation depended on me knowing that stuff I'd hire someone who could take care of it for me while I focused on what I do best."

"You're kidding."

"Hell, no. I'd hire a chef or—"

"No, I mean, you're kidding about having no interest in food."

He shrugged powerful shoulders beneath the white shirt. "Never understood the whole hype. I mean, it's science. Eat enough to give you energy but not so much to make you fat. Not too much of any one thing so you're getting the right nutrients. I don't buy all this fiddling around and agonizing over whether something's got Omega 3 or which herb to put on groundhog. Just don't see the point."

She let out an unexpected laugh, and her whole body hummed with the relief. "Can't say I've ever had to think about which herb goes with groundhog."

He moved onto the freeway, and the car leapt to life. "My point is, you're in a whole pile of trouble and with the threat of this tape it's only going to get worse. Let me look after your image for the next two weeks and if by that time I haven't turned everything completely on its head, not only will D and D pay back every cent of the contract fee, we'll triple it."

The possibility of having someone—especially someone as take charge and sure of himself as Blake Matthews—sharing some of this burden caused her to sigh softly as every part of her relaxed. "To be honest, I don't have any energy left. I should be in TV studios talking about my new ice cream brand, not dealing with this. I thought that in settling out of court as we did, it'd be the last I heard of the complete lie that I sexually harassed Trent."

"Then someone gave you terrible advice. Sex sells, and when there's a hint of sexual misconduct from someone as well-known as you, it's like a license to print money for TV shows and magazines for years after the event, and don't get me started on how long it will be in the cloud." He shot her an ironic smile. "Interest in your sex life will follow you around like toilet tissue stuck to your shoe for a long time yet, Kirin. And don't get me wrong, attention is exactly what your business is going to need in the coming months. The good kind, not the destructive kind."

Her sex life? God, if he only knew how long it had been.

Blake held a hand out, palm up, as if he spoke the obvious truth. "The fact you settled with Trent gave people the feeling that because there was smoke there must be fire. That you were hiding a secret, sexy side. Trying to deny that by reinforcing, or even playing up, your current conservative image would not only take too long, it's not what your public wants. If we play to their image of you as a confident, take charge thirty-something business woman, they'll feel you're finally being honest." He drummed his fingers on the steering wheel. "We could even find the sex tape and expose it."

She nearly shot out of her seat as she swung her body toward him. "What!? You've got to be kidding! That's the last thing we'll do. Absolutely, unequivocally, no way are we looking for that tape, let alone exposing it! And I've told you there can't be a tape. I will not play Trent's game anymore."

For a beat, then two, he was silent. "Excellent. Just the sort of passion we need from you. So, you've decided to let me turn your public image around?"

She sighed and focused on the windshield as she shook her head. "I really don't see how you can fix my image after this news. And I don't see how playing into the public's impression of me as a secret sex fiend would do anything but harm my reputation more."

"That's because you're a chef and I'm an image expert."

She twisted toward him. "I don't want this dragging on, Blake." Her voice quavered. "I can't face this day after day with things popping up out of the woodwork." Her throat closed as she fought a new well of tears.

"Give me two weeks."

She swung her gaze back to his face and blinked the dampness away. "You think you can make a difference in two weeks?"

"What would you most like to happen? If you could turn anything around, what would you do?"

She didn't need to think. "I'd like to stop getting abusive phone calls, DMs, texts and emails for starters."

"And?"

She breathed slowly, the prospect that he could make all this go away, almost too good to believe. "I'd like to put my side of the story properly to someone who cares about the truth, someone who the public respects and who'll tell the *real* story of what happened to my marriage, to me..."

"More."

Although it sounded impossible, it felt good to say all this out loud, and her heart beat stronger. "I want to cater a major function in town and have everyone rave about my food again. I want to have my publisher return my calls, my debts to stop mounting. I want to give back to all those people who've believed me but who've suffered through this complete nightmare too."

"That's quite a list for a superhero in two weeks, let alone a PR guru. I'd need my outside undies on for that."

The corner of her mouth tugged in a wobbly grin. "You think it's asking too much?"

"Not at all. But if we're to pull it off, you'll have to give me your full cooperation, and by that I mean no arguing with me about clothing choices, appearances, tweaks I might make to your presentation in all areas of your life. I'll own your image for two weeks and you'll put your trust in the understanding that you're the expert on eggplants and I'm the expert on image."

Kirin leaned back against the seat again, as a strange mix of relief and trepidation cycled through her. Could he really do that for her? "And what if we've achieved none of those things at the end of two weeks?"

Blake turned to her, his perfect lips quirking in a half-smile. "With me in your corner? Not a chance of that happening."

3

---

*S*econds after Blake had pressed the old-fashioned bell the next afternoon, the door to a modest house in Santa Monica swung open and Kirin Hart smiled at him.

Today her blond hair was pulled tightly away from her face and lay as a braid over one shoulder. A soft, white blouse hid the curves he knew lay beneath, and a navy blue, knee-length skirt made her appear more like a middle school teacher receiving a parent for an interview, than the captivating woman he'd met across a kitchen counter days earlier.

The low-key outfit didn't mesh with the spark in her eyes, or the way she'd held herself when they'd first met. This was a woman of intriguing contradictions, and he couldn't wait to get to know her better.

"I was expecting you at five." Kirin stood aside to let him in. "Not half past. I can only give you an hour now."

He grinned and moved through the doorway into a light and airy hall. He was a little late, and it was clear she was going to make him work hard for what he needed—and he'd enjoy every minute of it.

An enormous palm-like tree sat in a bright pink pot, and along the wall a wooden table held vases and photo frames. He bent down to look more closely at the snaps, but she stood in front of him and held out an arm. "We can talk in the kitchen." He nodded. He loved the way she played the ice-queen businesswoman, but he'd seen tantalizing glimpses of a softer, more exciting Kirin and he couldn't wait to see that again.

"This will take more than an hour." He followed her down the hallway to a closed door at the end. "You'd better cancel your plans. And order us takeout."

"I'm sure an hour will be long enough," she said sweetly. "And I don't do takeout unless I've been run off my feet at work and that hasn't happened in a while." She opened the door and his ears were assaulted by a bark that was deep, loud, and ominous. It came from a dog that gave a new meaning to ugly.

"That's Dudley," Kirin said with a warm smile. "He doesn't like men much. Just don't make any sudden moves."

Incredibly, the mutt looked like a cross between a basset hound and a poodle, with his belly, ears, and even its jowls almost touching the floor. Its droopy eyes made it look as though it'd been playing poker all night long and wasn't amused at being interrupted.

"That's enough, Dudley," Kirin said in a sweet voice and the old dog stopped barking and looked as if it might cry.

She moved behind the kitchen counter and turned to him. "Iced tea?"

He put his laptop on the raised counter, one eye on Dudley to make sure he was obeying Kirin. "No thanks. Hate the stuff. I had a grandmother from England who made pots and pots of hot tea all day, every day. Makes me gag just smelling it. I'll have a burger and fries when you order."

"I could squeeze you some juice." She pointed to a fruit bowl. "Or get you something stronger? I'm sure this won't run into dinner time."

He'd had a hell of a day setting things in motion for this project. "Sure, something stronger would be good."

She reached up on tiptoe to open a cupboard. "You'd be a liquor drinker." His eyes were drawn to her shapely calves as she stretched up. "Whiskey or vodka. It's all I have, I'm afraid." She suddenly twisted around and, caught off guard, he quickly swung his eyes back to her face.

"What makes you think I'm a liquor drinker?" He focused on pulling up a stool. "I don't have a rum nose, do I?"

She looked him in the eye and grinned. "What you said yesterday about food and how you didn't understand the hype behind it. If you feel that way about food I can't imagine you'll have a big appreciation for wine." She shrugged a shoulder. "And you mentioned something about not eating too much, so I guessed you weren't a beer drinker. Liquor is uncomplicated."

Watching her full lips move as she talked, a strange sense of déjà vu overtook him—Kirin calling the shots from the protection of a counter-top, just as she'd done on the first day. His mission today would be to break down a few of the physical barriers she had up. It screamed control, and she needed to pass some of that to him if they were going to get anywhere.

"You sure do pay attention. Whiskey, thanks."

She swiveled back to him, bottle in hand, and there was a softness in her eyes. "I like to think I'm a good listener."

She put the bottle on the counter and opened the refrigerator door. While she had her back to him, he quickly scanned the room. There was a low chest of drawers with more photos, and an enormous, shiny plant in a corner.

A sofa with some crazy-colored cushions looked out on the sunny backyard, and the framed sketch of a nude woman hung on a wall. Everything in his research had led him to expect someone far more conservative in the ways she'd express herself. He'd imagined beige drapes and plastic covering her couches. And if she were to have a dog, which he hadn't factored at all, he'd have picked it to be pedigree Labrador or a corgi, not the random-looking mutt slumped on his cushion in the corner. Interesting. "You live alone?" he asked as she turned around with a pitcher in her hand.

She opened a cupboard and took down two glasses. "My brother, Flynn, moved in for a few weeks after Joe died to help me cope with all the extra media interest, but apart from that I've been here alone for the last few years." She put the glasses on the counter and poured whiskey into one, ice tea into the other. "Dudley's the only company I need at home these days. I moved my mom from Iowa last year into an apartment a few blocks away. She likes to sit in my backyard and paint so I see her a lot." Reaching for a fluorescent lemon, she said, "I'm guessing you'll have your whiskey neat?"

Goddamn, this insight thing of hers was starting to spook him. He nodded. "You mean you've always lived here?" He took in the hand-knotted rug and what looked like a crazy collection of salt and pepper shakers on a shelf. "I'd have thought that with all the success you'd had, you'd have chosen somewhere with more… celebrity."

She sliced into the lemon skin. "Joe wanted to move to

Brentwood or the Hollywood Hills when we started making a lot of money. But this was the first place we bought when the business had begun to take off and I always felt safe here. I'd put in a great veggie garden and didn't want to leave it."

She reached across the counter and handed him the glass. As he took the drink, his hand brushed her little finger, and she pulled back. Soft pink tinged her cheek as she turned away. The chink in her previously solid armor was surprising.

"Let's take a look at my strategy plan," he said as he took the tumbler to the dining table. He hadn't looked forward to working with a client this much in… ever.

She hesitated a moment, then came around the counter and put a plate of pastry-looking things on the table. "They're pesto twists. Try one."

"No thanks, not hungry yet." He flipped his laptop open.

"I'm not hungry either." She picked up a pastry twist. "But these are so good." Eyes still on his face, she put it to her lips, and he quickly focused back on the table.

"So, the questionnaire I sent over this morning." He stared hard at the screen and imagined her lips wrapping around the stick and his throat dried. "We'll go through your answers and from that I'll detail our plan of attack."

He looked up to see her licking a pastry flake from her lip. And it was the sexiest thing he'd ever seen.

"I don't have the questionnaire."

His fingers stilled on the keyboard. "You haven't completed it?"

"No." She blinked once, twice.

He shrugged. "We'll start with what you've done and fill in the rest as we go. I'll record your answers and have them transcribed later."

She lifted her chin and cleared her throat. "I've done none of it."

"What?" He lifted his eyes and caught the determined resistance on her face. A challenging look that caused his pulse to spike.

A wisp of hair had slipped across her face and she flicked her head so it shifted. It was either a move of sexy self-assurance or barely disguised defiance. "I don't see why you need to know all these things about me." Counting off on her fingers, she drummed on the table. "Who my parents are, where I went to school, whether I vote Republican or Democrat." She held him still with her wild honey eyes. "What does that have to do with winning my public back?" She took another bite of the pastry thing and chewed slowly.

He leaned back in the chair, determined to focus on the question and not the sexily hypnotic way her mouth moved. "It has everything to do with it. I need to know who you are, what your values are. I also need to be told of any skeletons in your closet. If I don't know this stuff..." He paused until her gaze met his so she'd know how serious this was. "If I put my neck on the line for you and something comes and bites us in the ass, then we'll be screwed. I don't like being screwed."

She said nothing, just drew a pattern in the condensation forming on the delicate glass.

"I'll assume if you won't answer my questions, then there are things in your past you don't want revealed. If that's the case we're finished before we even get started."

She licked another pastry fleck from her top lip, and he shifted in his seat. "I don't know you. I've no reason to trust that you won't use my answers in a way that I hadn't intended." Her eyes were glossy. "What happened to me yesterday is an example of what some people will do with information about me. How do I know you're not one of them? Can't you just ask me those things in a normal conversation without being so clinical?"

He sighed and rubbed a hand across his jaw. He should've known she wouldn't give this stuff up easily. Especially after the TV debacle yesterday. Perhaps he'd given her the impression he'd be reasonable on this. Easy fix. "We have two weeks to get this done, and I need to know everything about you right now. Enough stalling."

"So, why don't you ask me?" She lifted the glass to her lips and drank. Her throat moved in small swallows, and the skin at the back of his neck heated. She drew her lips away and wiped her moist mouth with the back of her hand, all the while holding his stare. "And when I've answered something about me, you can tell me about you."

He frowned. "Why would you want to know anything about me?"

"Because I need to *trust* you. I've been hurt by a lot of people in the last few months, Blake, and I need to protect myself." She rolled her lips together. "If I'm going to put my whole life, my whole future in your hands, I deserve to know who I'm giving that privilege to."

He grinned and reached for his own glass. This power play was so damn sexy he might get put off his game if he wasn't such a professional. "You mean you didn't Google me as soon as I left your kitchen that first day?"

The skin at the corner of her mouth crinkled as her lips lifted and eyes sparkled. "Of course I did, but all I found were pictures of you in ads for European watches and fast cars." The curve of her mouth grew. "Oh, and a couple for designer underwear. Apart from a few references to a PR business in New York, there was very little. Nothing about a family. Or where you came from."

Blake focused back on the laptop and hit the record button. She didn't need to know anything about him. He changed the subject. "Tell me how you met Joe Hart." He turned back to face her. "Were you happy in your early days?"

She paused for a moment and blinked as she stared past him. "No, I wasn't happy. My mother, my little brother Flynn, and I lived in a rented trailer. Momma was a waitress at the local truck stop and she'd often work double shifts to make enough money. Life wasn't easy, and I felt responsible."

"How did you get into cooking?"

She held the glass in both hands and stared at it. "We were struggling financially, so when Flynn was old enough to look after himself, I went to work at the diner where Momma was." Her chest rose, then fell. "It took me about two seconds to get fed up with the silent, and not so silent, abuse the waitresses suffered, so I asked to be moved to the kitchen."

He nodded. "And you fell in love with food and nourishing people and the rest is history."

She shook her head and looked up at him. "Far from it. I fell in love with Joe. He was the owner's nephew and had been on the grill since he was twelve. I was seventeen when I met him and he was twenty-five. I fell for him. Hard and fast."

Blake raised an eyebrow, intrigued by her tone rather than the story. He'd read about her past and had assumed the picture she'd give him would be gold-plated nostalgia. The weary edge to her voice and the tired look in her eyes suggested time hadn't gilded reality at all. "Was Joe a good chef?"

She shrugged. "Joe didn't love food the way I did, but he knew what people liked and could see we made a good team. Later on he was all about the presentation, the package, and he believed that with our down-home dishes, our work ethic, and our husband and wife brand, we could sell a whole lifestyle to people. And we did. Until it turned out he'd been living a double life and. . . you know the rest."

"And you believed those things too, initially?" He took a sip of the warm whiskey.

Lifting her chin, her eyes tracked out toward the garden. "I just wanted to get away from the diner and the feeling that that was all there was in life. Joe offered me the world back then, and I believed he'd give it to me."

"Must've been tough when he died."

"Of course it was tough." Her breath caught. "I'd been with Joe since I was seventeen and he died when I was thirty-two. For so long I'd looked to him to tell me who I was." She clasped her hands together on the table. "We'd grown apart years before he died and he'd had a string of other relationships. We were nothing more than business partners for much of our time together—but funnily enough, he was still the one I wanted to impress, the one I depended on. The whole persona of 'Cooking with Hart' was down to Joe and his vision for our brand and it was very successful."

Blake leaned forward and rested his arms on the table. "And where do you see that brand now? Do you believe you can save it?"

Her voice hardened, and her eyes sparked. "I *have* to."

"Why?"

"Because I owe a lot of people a lot of money now. The

only way I know how to pay them back is to do what I've always done. Cook." She trapped her lip between her teeth. "If enough people could understand the real me, then they'd realize I am a good person, that I do have integrity."

He didn't reply until she looked at him again, her soft brown eyes glittering. "And who *is* the real you, Kirin? Is it the female part of 'Cooking with Hart', or is it someone different?"

"What do you mean?"

He undid a button on his cuff and rolled up one sleeve, and then the other. "You said that although you loved food, you followed along with Joe's plan for a celebrity cooking team. Are you sure you're that persona still?"

She didn't answer, so he reached into his laptop case and pulled out a pile of papers. "These are the latest ads, cookbook covers, and product frontages for the 'Cooking with Hart' brand. What do you see?"

She reached for the pile and slowly flicked through. "Just me."

He pointed to the one closest to him. It was an ad for cooking stock, with Kirin holding a bowl of soup. "White t-shirt and blue jeans." And the next. "Beige shirt dress and sensible shoes." And another. "Hair in a bun."

"Your point?" She hooked him with sparking eyes. God, he loved it when she did that.

"This isn't the real you at all. You're trying to fight to preserve an image that doesn't exist. The way you look in these pictures is the same way you looked fifteen years ago when you started 'Cooking with Hart'. And it's such a contrast to the person you really are, that I don't buy this." He tossed one of the pictures aside. "And since the sexual harassment allegations surfaced, your public doesn't either."

One fine eyebrow rose. "How do you know this isn't the real me?"

"The clothes you wear, the way you fix your hair, none of it matches the look in your eye, the way you hold yourself, the confidence that shines from you."

She grinned. "A look in my eye? Must've squirted some lemon juice in it."

He ignored her attempt at being dismissive again. "When I found you that first day, I saw someone who cooked and spoke with fiery passion, not someone who wanted to live life through reserved, buttoned-down order like this." He swept the pictures aside.

"I'm not an image, Blake. I'm just Kirin. I wear what I've always worn, fix my hair the way that feels best."

He leaned in. "We're all an image and you can choose whatever you want it to be. In my old life I could be a sheik in an advertisement for hotels one minute, a soldier in a TV campaign for military recruitment the next. An image doesn't need to be real, but it needs to be believable, and from what I can see in front of me right now…" He flicked a hand toward the pile of ads. "I don't believe this image of you anymore."

Her hand moved to her throat. "So what image *should* I be portraying?"

"We need to drag you into the twenty-first century." He steepled his fingers under his chin. "Update you in every area. Your image should reflect who you are now—a modern, sexy, single woman who's not scared to be herself."

Kirin tapped a fist against her lips. "Won't that just play into people's ideas of me as some sort of cradle-snatching cougar?"

He put his hands flat on the table, energized by this assignment, and by the possibility of working so closely with the intriguing woman in front of him. "If we give them an image of you that fits more closely with what they already believe, then your brand becomes more authentic."

"Even if it's not?"

He leaned back in his chair. "Am I wrong in thinking the real Kirin Hart is far more sensual than these photos would suggest?"

She sat back and eyed him with a similar look to the one Dudley had given him when he arrived. "I'm guessing my opinion's not going to cut much with you."

"You're right. Your opinion doesn't matter to me right now, what does matter is saving you and your business before it's too late. To do that we're going to expose your sensuality to the world."

A heated flush swept across Kirin's chest and fanned up her neck. This confident, sexy man, who she'd only known a few days, was talking about how sensual she was, and it was unnerving.

Her throat tightened. Of course it was. It was the same flattering talk Trent had started out with, and he'd wanted something from her, too. A promotion. And when she passed him over for it because he wasn't up to the job, he'd claimed sexual harassment. In the last weeks and months she'd faced some harsh lessons about men who said what they needed to get what they wanted from her.

"I think you're forgetting something." She strengthened her tone. "I'm thirty-four years old. A different decade to you, I'm guessing. I'm not comfortable showing a sensual side to my public. Maybe in the privacy of my own home, where I couldn't be judged, but even then it's not—"

"That's ridiculous," he said bluntly, and leaned back in his chair. "And by the way, there's only five years' difference between you and me. Hardly figures. Your audience is mostly middle-aged people—men who want to marry you and women who want to *be* you. Cooking and sex go together whether you like it or not and sexing you up will fit perfectly with the new image of you as a single, powerful woman."

"But why should I change?" It was fine for Blake with his perfect movie star face and his sense of cool style that had her rattled from the moment they'd met. He oozed sex appeal from every pore with no effort whatsoever, and she felt like a hot mess in comparison.

Blake's eyes widened. "Are you kidding me?"

She squirmed in her chair, uncomfortable with the incredulous look on his face and the fact he'd caught her staring. "I'm content having ordinary looks and an ordinary figure." He didn't need to know how much she hated her boobs or how her stomach had more rolls than a dinner basket. "I've made myself stand out through my cooking and my business, and I resent having to reinvent the way I look. Someone like you can pull it off because you're so..." She stopped and swallowed. "I mean you look... And people..."

He leaned back in his chair, a teasing smile at the edges of his mouth. "Go on."

"You have sex appeal in spades," she said in a rush. "It almost drips off you without you even trying. I don't know how to do that. Don't think I could ever get that right."

"Kirin." Blake's stare burned right through her. "Trust me when I say you have sex appeal just waiting to be unleashed." Now the burning was working its way down her body. A response wouldn't come so with a tremble in her fingers, she took a quick sip of the tea in an effort to cool herself.

"Your audience has made you who you are. They've stayed loyal, bought your products and cookbooks, they've believed everything you've told them. But you took that trust for granted. When you did that back room deal with Bray they felt cheated, as though they didn't know the real you, as though you hadn't trusted them enough to tell them what really happened."

"But I had no choice." Everything bottled inside threatened to overtake her, but she wanted Blake to understand what she'd been through. "If I hadn't settled with Trent, then who knows what else he might've done."

He shrugged a strong shoulder. "None of that matters. We can't give your fans who they had before because that conservative, controlling woman can't be trusted. We need to give them a fresh Kirin, a confident Kirin, a Kirin Hart who says, 'Yes, I've changed since my husband died, yes, I know who I am now, yes, I'm the sexy, single woman you all thought I was, and you can have confidence that this is the real me.'"

He pushed his chair back. "Stand up." As he moved to her side of the table, the determined look on his face sending a sizzling thrill through her. "We need a decent mirror."

An image of them standing together in her bedroom seized her insides, and she cleared her throat. Never again would she allow boundaries to be crossed by an employee, especially not a younger male one who was having this effect on her. "The bathroom. There's a mirror in the bathroom."

"It's full-length?"

No way in hell was she going to take him to her bedroom.

"Not quite, but it'll do."

"After you."

She led the way, and when they were in the white-tiled sanctity of her bathroom, he ordered her in front of the wall mirror.

She raised her eyes. In her slip-ons, she was no more than five-four. Of course she'd done her hair this afternoon and, truth be told, she'd even put on some mascara in anticipation of his visit, but in contrast to Blake Matthews's casual and heart-stopping perfection, she looked like something even the cat wouldn't drag in.

He was so far from the male models she'd seen showcasing skinny jeans and neck scarves on the cable fashion channel. His was the sort of look you'd see on an ad for fire service recruitment, or selling a European car—all chiseled jaw and perfectly tended muscle.

"I'm going to be brutally honest now, so be prepared." She steeled herself for his criticisms. "You've been part of a husband and wife team for a long time. You met Joe when you were a teenager, and you've kept the same conservative, dependable image for years. The reason things have turned so drastically is that you're still selling yourself as part of a wholesome duo when you're something totally different now."

She leveled her gaze at his reflection. "Of course I'm different. I know the business can't be the same as when Joe was here, but I think I've always presented myself honestly."

He placed a hand on each of her shoulders and warmth radiated through the upper part of her body like midday sun on naked skin. "You don't have to counter everything I say. Just listen. Your public wants to love you, but they also need to see you as your own person. Not half of a whole. You're an incredibly smart, hardworking woman in her mid-thirties who has every right to be who you want to be, but your public can also see that you're a contradiction."

His sexy-low voice bounced off the bathroom walls and danced sweetly in her ears. "Because you've changed since Joe died, you need to show that in a physical sense—in the way you look, the way you speak, the things you do. You need to give your public confidence that they can believe in you again. They need to see you as Kirin Hart, not as part of a relationship, imagined or otherwise."

She moistened her lips, head spinning with Blake's proximity and the deeply personal nature of his words. "I'm not sure which is the real me. Joe had some firm ideas about how we should look, and what we should say in public. He even had our charities picked out to reflect the values we were trying to present."

He smiled, the dimple in his cheek deepening. "And because you'd paid for the marketing campaigns, you had no opportunity to develop into the independent woman you grew to be. Kirin, it's important the public senses your new confidence. But we have to get rid of the narrow, lewd way you've been portrayed in the media since the Bray debacle. Image starts at the shop front, at the way you present your-self physically." He picked up her braid and ran his thumb slowly over the end. "You like this?"

She smiled ruefully. "I'm guessing that means you don't."

He surveyed it, then squared his gaze back at her in the mirror and shrugged. "It's fine. But fine doesn't cut it for you anymore. You want to reinvent yourself? We'll start with your hair. We'll cut it a lot shorter, perhaps a bob, and we'll color it. Your brown eye, blond hair combination is stunning but we'll emphasize it even more."

Heat touched her cheeks. The compliment was given in such a matter-of-fact way, but coming from Blake, it had the power to hold her still.

"You don't need much makeup but there are some necessities." He drew a finger through the air near her cheek and she held a breath. This was excruciating. Thrilling and excruciating. "Lash lift to accentuate your eyes, some bronzer to highlight your killer cheekbones, and lip gloss. Never leave the house without lip gloss."

She grinned. "I've never known a man to be so knowledgeable about hair and make-up."

"I won't apologize for it. Society assumes heterosexual men have no interest or understanding about image, which makes me so in demand and my clients so satisfied. This approach is real, it works, and there's no one more experienced than me to provide you with it."

There was something so powerfully magnetic about him. Some might call it arrogance or cockiness, but whatever it was, it was impressive, and made her weak at the knees. For the last two years she'd been in charge of everything and everyone around her, and it felt so good to have someone else take control for a change.

She lifted the collar of her blouse. "So, what about my clothes?"

He stepped away as his gaze raked her body, sending a shower of sparks through her. With his eyes, he peeled off each layer of clothing, leaving her skin humming.

"Feminine but sophisticated is what we want. By representing you as sophisticated and confidently sensual, your public's going to realize that they've got you all wrong. That there's no way someone as confident and together as you would've risked her business for a cheap thrill with a low-life like Trent Bray."

Suddenly uncomfortable with this intimate talk, she stepped away so she could see him properly. "How do you know this stuff works?"

"Experience. Watching prominent people through history." He folded his arms and lounged against the tiled wall. "Take Bill Clinton. Being linked to sex and intrigue could've killed his presidential career, but because his image was managed so carefully, he became more popular than ever."

"Were you even alive when Bill Clinton was around?"

He chuckled. "That's my point. Sex scandals live to infinity but it's the way they're handled that determines how they affect someone's reputation."

"You're saying he had image advisors who wanted to play the sex angle up?"

"Put it this way, if Clinton's image advisors had tried to make him look more conservative, more closed than before the incident, people would've seen through the lie. What they did was make him look sexier, more confident, and instead of a slightly academic and earnest president that he could've been, he became a charismatic and sexy president who people, especially women, fell in love with all over again. And it's resulted in him being one of the most loved presidents in history. Wouldn't you like a piece of that for yourself?"

"There's one significant difference between me and Bill Clinton."

Blake lifted an eyebrow.

She beat her index finger in the air. "I did not have sexual relations with that man."

He let out a belly laugh. "You know," he said, shaking his

head, "it doesn't matter what the truth is, what matters is how we deal with people's perception of it."

Suddenly, the laughter and warmth in the room vanished. "It matters to me. It twists my gut that anyone might believe I could sexually harass someone."

"Of course it does, but just as with Clinton, the public doesn't really care. They just want to believe in you again." He crossed his arms. "When I was fifteen I was discovered by a photographer who was vacationing in our town. After taking some shots and sending them to an agency in New York, I ended up signing a modeling contract and moving to the city a few days after my sixteenth birthday. From then on I learned pretty quickly how to give people the look they wanted. We're going to give people the look they want for you."

This was the first glimpse of the man behind the God-like face and body, and she had to know more. "Where are you from?"

"A small town in Oregon." His focus turned back to her clothes. "What sort of fabric is this skirt? You won't want to stand next to a naked flame."

"That must've been hard for your parents, letting you go so far from home on your own into such an unknown world."

Something flickered in his eyes. "We're talking about you, not me." He touched her back, and a shower of sparks radiated through her. "We'll move on to clothes tomorrow."

A mask had slipped across his face at talk of his past and although she wanted to ask him more about himself, she decided to save her questions for later.

"I've asked one of my old friends, Lucy, to dress you in her studio tomorrow," he said. "She'll ask what sort of fabrics and looks you like as well as giving you some new styles to consider. I've organized to have your hair done by a great stylist, too. He's a bit of an enigma and will only see you in his salon, so we'll do that the following night. I'll pick you up at eleven for the meeting with Lucy tomorrow but be prepared to spend the rest of the day with me."

A sudden swirl of dread forming in her stomach, Kirin folded her arms. This was all happening so fast. "What if I don't like the clothes and the hair? What if I can't carry off this whole new image? I might end up looking like a complete idiot." She bit her lip. "I don't know if I can be confidently sensual."

"You shouldn't worry so much, Kirin. And about the confidence? You've got it already. We just need to tease it out a little. "

She blinked, but he held her gaze, and her heart tripped. "Tease it out, how exactly?"

"You have all the tools to be confident already, but to show that inner strength, people need to see the window dressing." His voice dropped. "That's all we're doing. We're just aligning the outside to the Kirin Hart you have in here."

He reached out as if to place his palm across her heart but stopped in midair, and in the seconds that passed, she felt the room crack with her lightning desire for him.

She took a hurried step back and rearranged her blouse. "See you tomorrow, then." And when he gave her one of his devastatingly slow smiles, she wished the floor would open up and swallow her whole.

How on earth would she cope with having Blake Matthews so close and so intently focused on her for two whole weeks?

Kirin: *Hey girls, anyone else having the week from hell?*

Gwin: *Beelzebub has nothing on the crazy person I turned into this week. I hope things have been better for you, Ellie.*

Ellie: *Complete pants over here as well. One of the few things that's getting me through the week is knowing that I can talk to you guys about it every day.*

Kirin: *Same!*

Gwin: *K, I nominate you to go first. Tell us about it.*

Kirin: *I have a new image consultant and despite all my efforts I haven't broken him yet.*

Ellie: *HE?! That's fresh. What's he like?*

Kirin: *If you can imagine a smooth assassin in a freshly laundered suit who smells like a god then that's kinda what he's like.*

Gwin: *A hot guy spending every waking hour with you? I'm struggling to find the problem here, K.*

Kirin: *Okay, I want to be completely up front with you guys. Part of the reason things have been pretty tough lately is that I had a sexual harassment suit brought against me. I run a big company and a guy who was overlooked for promotion decided he'd get back at me by making up some lies. This image consultant's job is to redo my image so I can try to rebuild my career.*

Gwin: *That's awful!*

Kirin: *It has been and still is, to be honest. Look, I know you guys don't really know me, but if there's nothing else you believe about me in any of these chats, please just know that none of the accusations were true. I was only alone in a room with the guy once, but his influence on my life right now is frightening.*

Ellie: *Oh wow, that's pretty intense.*

Kirin: *It's been a pretty awful few months. This whole new image thing is supposed to turn my fortunes around, but this new consultant really has his work cut out for him. What's been happening with the move plans, Gwin?*

Gwin: *So, I've finally applied for a job in the city!!!*

Ellie: *Your sister's agreed it's time to leave?*

Gwin: *Yes, I was really struggling to get Ava to agree until Rosie, my niece who I live with, was escorted home by the police —drunk. She's not even thirteen, for God's sake.*

Ellie: *Oh, wow. That's tough.*

Gwin: *My mom's trying to blame a bad crowd and my sister not putting enough limits on.*

Kirin: *Any truth in that?*

Gwin: *Yeah, maybe. Life hasn't been easy for my sister. She had a baby when she was still at school and adopted him out and ever since then it's like she's trying to run from herself, you know?*

Ellie: *So Rosie is Ava's daughter?*

Gwin: *Yeah, she had Rosie only a couple of years after her son, so that's why my mom and I are around to help. Ava can be pretty wild still, and I think that's starting to have an influence on Rosie. I'm just relieved to be finally making some progress. Anyway, enough about me. What's happening with the project, Ellie?*

Ellie: *I've emailed all the owners of the houses on the beach to tell them they need to renovate. It's a really long story, but basically the houses are all old and neglected and damaging the surrounding environment with rusted pipes and stuff. The council will repossess the houses if nothing's done. It would be such a shame if that happened.*

Kirin: *That sounds like a lot of progress. What's so bad about the week?*

Ellie: *I realized that one of the houses is sill owned by a guy I haven't seen since we were eighteen.*

Kirin: *The ghost story you were telling us about from last week?*

Ellie: *Yeah, part of that story. He lives in the States though,* *thank goodness, so not much chance of him coming back here. Having him around would be the last thing I need.*

Gwin: *Still tough to relive that stuff, though. Was he a first love?*

Ellie: *Something like that. What's the name of this super model image consultant, K?*

Kirin: *Blake. I like to think of him as Doomed Blake. There's no way he's going to turn my image around in two weeks, like he's promising.*

Ellie: *Or he could Stud Muffin Blake or Beautiful Blake. I'm going to call him BB for short.*

Kirin: *He's younger than me and effectively my employee so he's COMPLETELY OFF LIMITS Blake!*

Gwin: *Oh crap, I see. That would be a complete and total failing in the image department, wouldn't it?*

Kirin: *Totally. And that's apart from the fact that I can't imagine dating for the next thousand millennia or so.*

They carried on chatting for the next fifteen minutes, and Kirin marveled at the fact that these two women who didn't know her at all could be so supportive and caring. It was as if the armor she'd bolted so firmly over herself since Joe's deceits were loosening.

Ellie: *Okay, goals for tomorrow? Mine is to get together a sort of CV about my landscape architect work so that all the people that remember me as a freckle faced ten-year-old have some belief in the project I'm managing. You, Gwin?*

Gwin: *Mine is to put out some more job applications and talk to my mom about how important it is that Ava and I move with Rosie to the city to give her more opportunities. K?*

Kirin: *I'm going to think nun-like thoughts about Doomed Blake, keep my snarky mouth shut when he's trying to give me clothes and hair advice, and to keep trying to dig my reputation out of the gutter and back to where I dreamed it could be.*

4

"Don't worry, Blake's often late." Lucy Evans, the stylist Blake had arranged, grinned as she hung brightly colored clothes on a rack in her large and airy studio. "Unfortunately, I have another client across town and she screams like a banshee if I'm a second late so I'll need to leave by one."

"I'm so sorry he's not here." Kirin checked her phone and tapped her ankle against the side of the chair. Twelve forty-five. She'd been talking cooking and clothes with the gorgeous and funny Lucy for nearly an hour and Blake's absence was embarrassing. He'd sent a driver instead of picking her up as they'd arranged, but she hadn't imagined waiting this long. He'd been late yesterday, too, and it was starting to annoy the hell out of her. Was he just rude, or was he fitting her original stereotype for a self-absorbed ex-model?

Lucy swiped the air with a silky-looking scarf, her silver-blond curls bouncing as she shook her head. "Blake still thinks he's the international divo who can turn up when and where he wants. Luckily everyone forgives him 'cause he's so freakin' gorgeous."

Kirin swallowed and tapped her foot a little harder. She'd lain awake last night, thinking far too much about how freakin' gorgeous Blake Matthews was. That dimple near his mouth, the smooth tan of his cheek, the spark in his eye when he'd reached out to touch her yesterday.

Her mouth dried, and she cleared her throat. She was being ridiculous. He was her employee, just as Trent Bray had been. A younger employee, and she'd never let her guard down in the same way ever again.

"Something important must've come up if he sent a car instead of picking me up." She did her best not to show the disappointment she'd felt when the driver had turned up and told her about the change of plans. It might've been fire, but when they'd pulled into Lucy's parking lot, the driver mentioned that a car had followed them for much of the journey and it had her on edge. Staying home so much lately seemed to have bored the photographers who'd trailed her when the scandal was at its peak. She hoped they weren't starting up again.

"Oh, Blake's so mysterious. He could be up to anything." Lucy picked up a soft blue dress and clutched it to her chest. "I would've murdered for a night with him once." She tossed her head back and closed her eyes. "We worked on a magazine shoot in Greece one summer and I can't tell you how incredible he looked. Not just in the final pictures, but on the whole trip. That face, that body. His abs make you want to play him like a harp." Her eyes sprang open. "Have you seen his most famous ad—the one for Birmingham underwear? I've got it somewhere." She looked around as if she might have multiple copies ready to produce in a second.

A detailed description of it was coming, whether Kirin had seen it or not—she could tell by the look of anticipation on Lucy's face. Shifting in her seat, every part of her heated as Lucy spoke breathlessly.

"Those little white shorts against steely tanned thighs, his hair slicked back and his body gleaming . . . and the way he's leaning over that girl, his lips starting to open... Ahhh... Every time I saw that ad I imagined it was me he was about to touch. And I bet he looked even better without any clothes on."

"You think?" Kirin's voice squeaked on the question.

Suddenly, Lucy's wide gaze swung to her. "Oh, God, you're not dating him, are you? I'm so sorry, Kirin. Sometimes my mouth just opens and dumb stuff spills out like it's sick of being in my head. I should've been more professional."

Kirin crossed her legs and tried to look nonchalant. "Me?" She brushed at imaginary lint on her gray leggings. "No, we're not dating. He's helping me out in my business, that's all." She smiled back at Lucy. "You should ask him out. You two would look great together. You must be similar ages." Suddenly Kirin felt every single one of her thirty-four years.

Lucy shrugged and hung the dress up before bending to get something from a large cardboard box. "He's dated drop dead gorgeous women in the past. And don't take it personally, him not asking you out, because he's wary of celebrities."

Nonchalance gone, Kirin twisted toward Lucy. "What do you mean, he's wary of celebrities?"

"Oh, he loves *working* with them. Of course he does. It's his business. He knows how to talk their talk, flatter them the way they like to be flattered." She lowered her voice a notch as she pulled a string of pearls from the box and laid them on a display stand. "He used to be in the glossy magazines all the time, especially when he was dating Ellen Carzolo. You know, the actress in the movie, Bluebird Bayou? But people thought she dumped him because he was jealous of how famous she became. Some say they were secretly engaged, and that she was devastated when he dumped her. You never see him with famous people in public anymore. Well, apart from working with them, of course. Which is what he's doing with you."

So he didn't like to be seen with celebrities? And he told them what they wanted to hear through sweet talk and flattery? Kirin sat straighter in the chair. Why should it matter to her? She only had to work with Blake for another two weeks, and then she wouldn't need to see him again. He'd be gone, and she'd be back to coping with all this on her own. She folded her arms across her stomach, the heavy dread that had been missing the last couple of days back with a vengeance.

"He's the perfect person to give you a makeover, though," Lucy said, beaming. "I've helped him style lots of different people and he really knows how to deliver a package that makes an impact. You'll end up looking sensational." Her voice softened. "I know things have been tough for you lately and it's sometimes hard to focus on things like presentation when our lives are a mess." She stopped. "Not that I don't think your presentation. . . I mean I *understand* why you've always dressed the way you have." She turned to Kirin, and her face fell. "Oh Kirin, I'm sorry. Mouth open. . . dumb stuff again. I didn't mean—"

"It's fine, Lucy. Really." She smiled. "You're right, I haven't been looking after myself enough lately. Which is why I need the help of someone as gorgeous and stylish as you."

Lucy took a relieved breath. "I saw you on the Larry

Williams show the other day. It was fabulous the way you took off when he started asking you about the sex tape. It took a lot of courage."

"Not really. I was just so shocked, I didn't know what else to do."

"Hi."

A door shut behind them, and at the mellow sound of Blake's voice, Kirin swiveled on her seat, her pulse inexplicably racing.

"Looks like I'm just in time." He strode across the room in a smart jacket and artfully faded jeans. "Great to see you, Lucy. Sorry I'm late." He leaned in and kissed her on both cheeks. "Your new studio's looking great!" A twinge in Kirin's chest at the sight of Blake kissing Lucy caught her by surprise. She was angry with him, that was all. Being late once was unfortunate, twice was plain bad manners.

"Oh, Blake." Lucy staggered a little as he released her. "Thank goodness you're here. Now that we're an hour late, I'm running into another booking. Just give me a minute and I'll get everything together so you can take Kirin through at your own pace."

As she hurried away, Blake shrugged out of his charcoal jacket and tossed it on a white couch as he pulled up a chair. "Sorry I didn't pick you up myself this morning. Stuff came up."

"Do you make a habit of making people wait?" She didn't care that her tone was icy. "You were late yesterday, too, and I'm not used to being kept waiting. I've given you fourteen days. Now there are only twelve and a half left. I've got better things to do than spend that time waiting around for you." She almost mentioned the driver's concern about being tailed, but she stopped herself. She'd handled that sort of thing without Blake Matthews, and if he wasn't going to be reliable, she'd continue to do it on her own.

He crossed his ankles and lifted a brow. "I've apologized. What more would you like me to do?"

She shrugged. "A simple text would be a start. Were you with another client?" Of course he was with another client. His intimate talk yesterday had convinced her she was something special. She wasn't. According to Lucy, that was all part of his business style.

"No." He pulled up a chair and eased himself into it. "There was an accident while I was out running, and I had to stay and help the women in one of the vehicles. I was thinking on the way here, though, that it's much better if we do this whole thing incognito, in the meantime, anyway."

Kirin blinked, trying not to feel guilty for where he'd been, and also trying not to notice the way his black shirt skimmed his torso, or the way he fitted so perfectly inside his jeans. She was angry with him and she wanted to stay that way, whether he'd been a good Samaritan or not. Far better for her concentration levels. "Incognito?"

"Yes." He leaned back a little and crossed his feet at the ankles. "First, it's best if your transformation looks like it comes from you as much as possible—that you've taken control and made choices for yourself. Secondly, it's important you're seen on your own or in the company of other women only. We don't need any paparazzi photos of you and me together. Or you with any man, for that matter."

"No men?" Blake's brisk business tone had caught her off guard, and she had to concentrate on what he was saying. "How long for?"

"Six to nine months, at least."

"I can't date for six to nine months? Not that I can

imagine dating at all any time in the next millennium, but still."

"Effectively, yes." He turned more fully to her. "Significant damage was done to your reputation through your relationship with Trent. We want everyone's focus to be on you alone now. There's no room for anyone else in the picture."

Her blood chilled, and she sat back. "There *was* no relationship with Trent. I've told you that."

He fixed sea-green eyes directly on her face. "Okay."

Didn't he believe her? The questioning set of his eyes suggested maybe not, and for some ridiculous reason it hurt.

"If we're to work together this closely, you're going to *have* to believe me," she said quietly. "There was no relationship, not even a hint of one. My dealings with Trent Bray were brief and nothing but professional."

He nodded. "I know."

Telling the celebrity what she wanted to hear.

He squared his shoulders. "I understand the details of what happened are important to you, but your public doesn't give a damn about reality. It's all about perception. We need to move on to how we can change the way they perceive you."

Her throat dried as she listened to his small talk about what they'd do today. Why should what he thought of her matter so much? He was right that they needed to focus on changing the public's perception. And for some unexplained reason, she wanted his perception of her to change, too.

"So, how do we do all this, then?" She shrugged off the gnawing in her belly and lifted her chin. "How do we meet to discuss strategies and visit places like this if we can't be seen together?"

He stood and walked to the clothes Lucy had hung on

the racks, and self-assurance pumped out of him. It didn't matter where he was—in an alleyway, a studio full of clothes, the kitchen of a woman he hardly knew—he possessed an overpowering sense of arrogance that left Kirin steaming, in all the good ways and all the bad. Never had she met anyone with such unapologetic, ball-breaking confidence.

"I'll send drivers to pick you up and take you to and from appointments and I'll meet you there as we did today." He picked up the hem of a dress and rubbed the fabric through his fingers. The movement was strong and sensual all at once.

Lucy's description of him half-naked in the magazine shot flashed through her mind, and she bit her lip.

"Any time we need to be together to talk strategy it'll be at your place or mine." He let the fabric fall. "And when we need to do something in public, we'll attend separately."

Part of her sagged with disappointment. In the days since they'd met, she'd had an underlying hope that Blake was going to be her knight in shining armor, the man who'd be there to protect her from all the nasty things that could happen. But of course he wasn't there to protect her, he was there to *change* her, and she'd get her head around that just as soon as she could stop imagining him in those tiny white boxers.

She shouldn't need a knight in shining armor. That was the whole point. Joe had been her protector for so many years, and it had been a large part of the reason she'd lost her own identity. It was time for Kirin Hart to be the one in the driver's seat—she would *not* be relying on any more men in her life. Especially not younger ones who thought they were the center of the universe.

Before she could reply, Lucy came hurrying back in with

another pile of boxes. "You said you wanted some shapely dresses in block colors, Blake, so I've put a few things together. I've teamed them with my choice of accessories but we can change anything you're not comfortable with." She turned to Kirin and put the boxes down. "The first thing we need to look at is your underwear."

Her blood ran cold. "Pardon?"

Lucy lifted the lid of the nearest box and pushed back some tissue paper. "I think we can find a much better bra for you. This one's not working with your gorgeous figure. I'll measure you up for something that fits and lifts you better." Lucy stepped forward and on reflex Kirin slammed her hands across her chest.

Blake rubbed a palm across his chin, head on one side as if appraising a brood mare or a new sports car. "Not shapewear though, Lucy? I want to keep Kirin's curves. If we're to believe she loves food and eats her own cooking, we don't want her looking too skinny. No tummy controllers. A natural-looking bra with decent support and a bit of push up will do it."

"Oh, really?" Lucy said, tilting her head as if to get a better view of the lumps and bumps, and Kirin automatically sucked her stomach in. "If you think it best—being au natural, I mean."

Kirin's head swung between the two of them as if she was at a tennis match.

Blake nodded. "Absolutely."

A piece of bacteria under a microscope or dog poo being inspected on the bottom of a shoe—that's what it felt like, being spoken over like this. As soon as Lucy turned to get something from the clothes rail, Kirin let out the breath and whispered to Blake, "We're not doing the underwear thing now, are we?"

His lips tipped in a grin and he whispered back, "I think we can let Lucy take care of that later. Let's just try a few of these dresses on and get a feel for the image. Unless you want me to take a look at your lingerie now?" He clasped his chin in his hand, head tilted. "I'd be more than happy to."

A rush of heat flooded Kirin's face, and she turned away. "I *bet* you would."

Five minutes later, Kirin was sucking in a breath again as Lucy buckled a thin white belt around her middle in the brightly lit fitting room. Blake sat only feet away behind a gauzy white curtain and already the roof of Kirin's mouth had dried, and her palms were damp at the thought of him scrutinizing her again.

Lucy stepped back and let out a sigh. "Oh, wow, Kirin. This look really suits, you. Truly. I have to admit when Blake told me I'd be working with you, I had my reservations. The last time I saw you in a photograph you were wearing one of those alligator clips in your hair and Crocs on your feet." Her whole body shuddered. "But you wear this updated fifties goddess look, beautifully."

Kirin grinned. She loved her alligator clips and wouldn't stop wearing them for anyone. Hesitantly, she stroked the soft fabric of the dress. It was light and comfortable, but seemed to hug every inch of her, and it was far too bright.

"Are you ready?" Blake called. "I seem to be growing roots out here."

"Ready," Lucy said, and before Kirin could prepare herself, she flung back the curtain.

As he lifted his eyes from the contract he was reading on his phone, the air seized in Blake's lungs. Kirin stood in front of him, hands crossed protectively in front of her, and he'd never seen anyone look more beautiful.

It wasn't the flyaway hair that had yet to be styled, or the belt she'd so vehemently argued with him about only minutes ago, it wasn't even the designer dress that hugged every perfect curve of her that caused him to stay motionless in the chair. It was the look on her face that he hadn't seen before. A hesitant, inquiring look that showed a spark within, as if a light had gone on and she was searching for how to make it brighter.

"I'm off now," Lucy trilled. "Sorry to leave you, Sweets, but I can't be late. You're in expert hands here, Kirin. I had fun today. Let's get together for a drink soon. I'll bring my sister, Pippa. She works magic with a makeup brush."

"I'd love that," Kirin called over her shoulder. "I'll text you."

Distracted by the vision in front of him, Blake lifted a hand to Lucy and he struggled for words. "How do you feel?" he finally asked.

She stared at herself in the mirror, shaking her head as her hands slid up and down the fabric. Her tongue poked out and moved slowly across her lips as she turned left, then right. Still, she said nothing.

"You look *great*," he finally said, his legs disobeying his desire to stand and be closer to her.

She frowned. "The fabric feels nice but..." Turning side on, she shook her head. "It makes me look far too busty." She pushed out her chest and then rolled her shoulders so it sucked back in. "I look like a bobble head."

Words refused to form as he battled for what to say. She most definitely did not look like a bobble head. She must know how stunning. . . and incredibly different. . . she looked, but he had to give her the impression she was making decisions just as much as he was. "You're in perfect proportion." He was still rooted to the spot, blood pounding through his veins.

"No, I don't think so." She swiveled on bare tiptoes. "It's not practical. Look at how this skirt sticks out. Imagine if that caught a gas flame."

He chuckled. "You'd need to be doing something pretty wild on a stove-top for that to catch alight."

A red tinge rushed across her cheeks, and she looked over her shoulder and frowned in the mirror. "I'd hate to spill spaghetti sauce down my front with this on." She looked back and her fingers brushed the skin exposed above her breasts and his mouth dried. The thought of her cooking in that dress, dripping a little sauce there and having it wiped—or licked—away, sent fire through his veins.

The dress, the sexiness of her bare feet, and the tiny belt at her waist had him mesmerized, but it was the way she held her chin higher, the tilt of her head as she looked at her reflection over her shoulder, that was doing him in.

He cleared his throat. "This is a great look for you. It's not cutting-edge fashion, but that's not what we want. We're after a look that defines you as an individual but still has you firmly in the role of domestic bliss creator. It's a perfect outfit for a cooking show."

"No, I'm not convinced." She dismissed everything he said with a flick of the wrist. He smiled inwardly at the return of controlling Kirin. "I'd have to wear high heels if I wore this and that would just look silly on a cooking set."

"You'd feel more comfortable in flats?"

"Flats are what I'd usually wear but they wouldn't look right with this, would they?"

He started looking through the boxes of shoes Lucy had left. "You don't like heels?"

"I do, but I'm five-four and Joe was only five-six. It never seemed fair to be towering over him, so I never wore them. And I was always worried about slipping in a TV studio."

"Try a wedge." He picked out a dove-gray shoe with pin pricks at the front and a tortoiseshell clasp at the side. "They'll give you the height and provide balance for the dress. And they're hot."

Kirin put her fingers to her lips as if physically holding back a smile.

"What?"

"No man I've ever met used the word wedge in relation to a shoe, let alone that it might be *hot*."

Trying to ignore the way her warm chuckle floated around the room, he took a shoe from the box and knelt. "Women love that I find shoes hot."

"Oh, I bet they do." She lifted her foot and the second it was in his palm, a bullet of heat shot up his arm. Her skin was silken-smooth, the delicate bones beneath making perfect ridges against his fingers.

Now. Put the shoe on now, a voice in his head said, but he didn't want to lose the sensation of her skin against his palm, and he stayed motionless.

"Blake?" she asked. "Are my feet too big? Oh, God, there's a bit of a bunion or something on the bottom of that one, too, isn't there?" She looked down and wiggled her toes. "How gross."

He slid his hand up to circle her smooth ankle. "No, your feet are perfect." He slipped the shoe over her delicate toes and placed her foot on the floor. "Although, when we've got you wearing peep toes, you'll be wanting a full pedicure."

What was this reaction to her all about? She didn't have

the looks or style of women he'd dated in the past. And he'd vowed to avoid relationships with anyone famous since the disastrous relationship with Ellen. Having paparazzi follow his every move, being constantly burned like an ant under a magnifying glass, had sworn him off the lifestyles of the rich and famous for good.

Apart from the fact that there was no way Kirin could be with any man—let alone one five years her junior after what had happened with Trent—he'd never go back to the moral vacuum of the celebrity lifestyle.

Talking about spicing things up and having to focus so closely on her lush figure and her sparkling eyes was bound to make him feel spiced up himself. And Kirin Hart was so much more than a client in need of a makeover. She was his ticket to owning the most powerful image consultancy in the nation. He wouldn't forget it and would rein in these responses to her before they got him in any trouble.

He buckled the shoe and drew himself to his full height. "Well?"

She turned side on and then to the front again, her lips pulling side-to-side, and then down in a pout. "No, it's not right. I can't see myself in this sort of thing. It's a major fail, I'm sorry."

"You've only tried on one dress. There are dozens more."

She tipped her head to one side. "Maybe something else would work." She tugged at one shoulder. "This is too revealing. Too sexy."

Sexy. She was damn right there.

"It's the perfect sort of sexy." He reached into his bag and pulled out a camera. "Just the right amount of skin showing, hugging in all the right places. Turn this way."

Immediately, her hands crossed over her chest. "What's that thing? What are you doing?"

"It's an instant camera. Prints instant photos. I use it to keep a record of the looks you've tried and we can find a common theme to the ones you like."

"Can I take a look?" He passed her the camera, and she turned it upside down. "Why don't you just use your phone and look at the photos later?"

"Because I've had fussy clients like you before and they get paranoid about having bad photos floating around. This way you can be in charge of 'possibles' and you can burn the 'no ways.'"

Her warm honey eyes narrowed. "You think I'm fussy?"

"I know you are, but I'll tell you how bad when we've tried some more outfits." He appraised her again. "What if you wore something around your neck, would that make you feel better about the neckline?"

"I don't know." She chewed her lip. "What did you have in mind?"

He put his hand low on his hips. "That necklace you were wearing the first day I met you would look good."

"The letter K?" A rose glow swept across her face. "You noticed that? I bought it the very first time I had enough money to start saving."

"It's good," he said. "Very you and a perfect complement to the dress."

She took a final look in the mirror. "I'm not convinced."

"Stand still." He lifted the camera to his eye, and before she could protest, clicked the button. "Got you," he said as she threw him a dark look.

He put the camera down and scanned the racks for more clothes. "Take the dress home and get used to it. It won't be too long before you find your new style. You won't need me for fashion advice after a while."

"I can't ever imagine feeling comfortable with all this."

Kirin picked up a pair of earrings and held them to her ears. "Colors and fabrics and what goes with what. It's enough to make my brain explode. I'm much happier working out which flavor goes with which. You just tell me how I should look and I'll be happy. Don't think I'll ever feel comfortable doing this on my own."

"You will." He stopped to look in her face. "When you've had some good feedback from the press and from your fans, you'll feel more confident about choosing this sort of thing to wear in public."

She took a deep breath and blew it out slowly. "I am kind of nervous about being seen in public like this. What if people see this sort of thing as confirmation that I'm a floozy? A lot of them still remember Joe and they might feel as though I'm cheating on his memory, changing the look."

"We're doing your public a favor. We're preserving the image of you and Joe before his infidelities—the good side of the 'Cooking with Hart' brand—for all time. Nothing will sully that memory now. Not another Trent Bray, not you wanting to move on and live your own life. All their memories of 'Cooking with Hart' will be locked in the past and they'll be ready to concentrate on the new you. Kirin Hart~Solo will be a great new brand. I'll talk with your marketing gurus about using it across the company. Have you and your independence as the focus from now on."

She folded her arms across her chest. "You certainly sound convincing."

"As I said, I'm the best there is. Just trust me when I say this is going to be the fastest way to turn things around."

She shrugged and something kicked deep in his chest. She didn't believe him, couldn't trust him after what had happened with Joe and then Trent. But she had no choice. For the first time since they'd met, she looked lost and vulnerable—and vulnerable was the last thing she needed to be seen as right now.

He cleared his throat. "Before we go along to the hair appointment, there's something I want to say."

"Sure."

He paused for a moment. "Just because I'm telling you to change what you wear and how you do your hair, it doesn't mean there's anything wrong with what you have already. If you were anyone else, you could keep your look and there would be no problem. You understand that, right?"

She nodded, but the look in her eyes told him she didn't believe him, that she was going along with what he asked her to do because she was desperate. For an inexplicable second, he wanted to reach out, pull her into his arms and tell her to relax, that she could trust him to get this right, and the feeling knocked him sideways.

Suddenly, the responsibility of what he was asking her to do hit home. This wasn't an actress looking for a dress for an awards show, or an IT geek wanting an updated look for a business launch. This woman's whole future depended on him.

Who was the vulnerable one now? There was no place for this sort of reaction to her. He needed to see her as his ticket to success. Nothing more. He cleared his throat. "When we've sorted the clothes out, you'll need to think about how you carry yourself. You have a tendency to slouch."

Her face dropped.

Yes, this was better. He had a job to do, and Kirin Hart's uncertainties and insecurities weren't going to stop him. "We have so little time for all this." Twelve days was all he had left to prove to the Dent and Douglas board that he could do this job and sweet-talking Kirin was obviously not working, so he owed it to her to bring in the big guns. He needed her on board with this makeover. Now.

Balancing a box of accessories in one hand, Kirin leaned her shoulder into the door of Lucy's studio and pushed out into the sunlight. Although Blake had kicked into cool, professional mode after she'd admitted her uncertainty with the way she looked, they'd eventually decided on some outfits for her to take home, and she felt a little better.

"Looks like we finished too early for your driver," Blake said as he walked towards her from a Tesla with the trunk open. "Wait in my car 'til he arrives if you like. I'll get the last of the shoes and lock up for Lucy."

When she arrived at his car, Kirin laid the box on the floor of the trunk and moved to the passenger side. She opened the door and, peering in, was immediately surrounded by the essence of Blake. Breathing in the clean-breeze scent of him, her stomach looped as she realized this was as close to the private side of him as she'd ever been. And she wanted more.

Leaning in to look over the passenger seat, she took in the charcoal overcoat laid across the back and the pair of running shoes beside it. Before she could see anything more, a voice from behind made her spin around.

"Well, look who it is."

Blood stopped, frozen in her veins.

Trent.

He stood at the front of the car, arms crossed, his face cut with a superior smile and his wraparound sunglasses making him look like a teenage punk. Gripping the door-frame, she pressed her back into the side of the car, and her jaw tightened. "What do you want, Trent? You're supposed to stay away from me."

He smirked. "Five hundred feet from your house, the agreement said. How can we talk when you're holed up there?"

Her throat dried. "You followed me here?"

"My eyes and ears are everywhere, Kirin, but I have far better things to do than follow you." He laughed. "Things like spend your generous settlement." A thin shoulder lifted, then fell. "At least, it *was* generous, but it seems to have dwindled. I was thinking that you might like to buy back the little tape I made of us and then we can call things even."

She lifted her chin as her heart pounded in her chest. He was revolting with his leering smile and his rude confidence. "There was no tape of us and you know it."

He stepped closer. "Everyone I've played it to *swear* it's you," he said. "The paisley scarf, the rolls around your middle, the old-fashioned jacket. . . couldn't belong to anyone else."

"Hey!"

Kirin turned to see Blake drop a pile of shoe boxes and come striding over to the car. Trent took a step back and suddenly the look on his face changed from confident to cowardly.

"Get the hell away from her," Blake said as he drew close. "Before I call the police."

Trent raised both his hands in the air. "Hey, no need to get nasty, brother. Kirin and I were just having a private discussion."

Blake turned to her. "Are you okay?"

She nodded, her pulse slowing. He gave her a reassuring smile, pulled out his phone, and took a photo of the scene.

In two more steps he was almost toe-to-toe with Trent,

and the intruder leaned back. "First things, first, I'm not your brother. Nor could I imagine anyone wanting to be a sibling of someone with so few morals."

Trent opened his mouth, but Blake continued. "Second thing is, you lost the privilege of having private conversations with Kirin a long time ago. I could have you arrested on about a hundred charges right now, including harassment, breaking a contract, intimidation." Blake's voice was low and with each word, Trent seemed to shrink a little. "But I'm the guy who doesn't like to waste police time with cowardly scumbags when I can deal with them myself."

He moved even closer, so that Trent had to step back. "I'm also the kind of guy who'll turn real nasty if I see or hear of you or your threats again. I have a photograph of you harassing Kirin, and if I hear word of any sex tape, any threat, or any contact with her again, I'll sue your ass. Are we clear?"

Trent rolled his tongue around in his mouth and finally stepped back. "You don't scare me."

Blake nodded. "Is that why your hands are shaking? They'll be quivering a lot more than that if my lawyers have cause to get involved."

Trent shoved both hands in his jeans pockets. "It's cool. No harm done."

"There will be harm done if you're not off this parking lot in the next ten seconds." And with that, Trent turned on his heels and hurried away.

Kirin placed her hand on the middle of her chest and finally breathed deep. "Thank you so much. God knows what I'd have done if you weren't here. How did you know it was him?"

"I recognized him from newspaper reports." He became more serious. "And you don't have to worry about me not being here. I'm going to be with you day in, day out, until Trent's just a nasty little memory. I get the feeling we won't be hearing much more from him."

As her driver pulled into the parking lot and Blake moved to talk to him, Kirin steadied herself with relief. It seemed that not only was Blake reliable, but for the first time since they'd met, she really felt he believed the truth about what had happened with Trent. And that meant more to her than she'd imagined.

5

"Colin isn't quite what you'd expect." Blake leaned in and whispered as they entered the back door of a city salon under cover of darkness the next evening. His scent of soap and sunshine filled her lungs, and she held her breath a little longer.

Like two spies, they'd met in the parking lot and were now making extra sure no one would see them arrive. Following the incident outside Lucy's studio, Blake had wanted to pick her up tonight, but she was determined Trent wouldn't influence their plans. Funnily enough, after the way Blake had dealt with him, she felt safer now than she had in a long time. Blake moved closer. His warmth jumped the space between them and heat spread up her neck. "He takes his work very seriously, but don't let him intimidate you."

He placed his hand on the small of her back, and the protective, solid gesture caused her nerves to jangle. The thought of being paraded before yet another image expert was causing her stomach to tie itself in knots. And it was more than her stomach that was all trussed up. Her thoughts were too.

It wasn't that she hadn't enjoyed looking at all the clothes and accessories Lucy had laid out for her yesterday, but she couldn't stop this ever-increasing feeling that she was losing part of herself each time they did this. She'd been trying on one of the tops when her mom stopped by this afternoon. Candi had been enthusiastic about Blake and Lucy's choices and had then detailed each wardrobe fail Kirin had ever had in her life. She knitted her fingers together in front. Having to be around Blake and his unwavering confidence in everything—especially what an image disaster she was—left her feeling out of control and floundering.

She still wasn't sure this was working. If it didn't go well at the hair salon tonight, she'd reconsider the whole deal and maybe ditch this constant feeling of inadequacy. But for now, her business and her entire career needed her to give it another try. And personally, was she ready to walk away from the chance of spending more time with Blake? She'd couldn't wait to talk to Ellie and Gwin in their weekly chatroom catchup about how she was feeling. They always helped.

Aside from the fact Blake seemed to get more and more jaw-droppingly gorgeous each time she looked at him, there was something intensely secretive about him, and she wanted to find out what it was. He often called her out on her need to control a situation, but he was the king of control, and part of her wanted to see what he'd be like when the designer boot was on the other foot.

What would he be like in the morning without his bespoke shirts and artfully mussed hair? Bare-chested and fresh from a shower, he'd smell like the ocean, his washboard abs with drops of water trailing . . . The image was so clear and so hotly distracting that as he stopped at reception, she almost ran into his back.

She blinked as the stark, white interior reflected halogen lights and chrome. It was bright enough to almost need sunglasses. A receptionist sporting an enormous pink beehive with tiny little bows all over it led them to a private room with puffy white leather couches. She took drink orders, then left to summon Colin.

"I don't want much off." Kirin fingered the ends of her hair. She'd sunk so far down into the luxuriously soft designer couch that she wasn't quite sure how she was going to get out. Everything about this place screamed inaccessible, intimidating style, and it made her stomach churn. "And I'm quite happy with the color right now." She twisted to get more comfortable.

"That's not a color." Blake spoke without looking at her. He sat on a fluorescent green plastic chair, elbows on his knees and flicking through a magazine. "That's a shade. And there's nothing that blends into the background more than a shade. Billie Eilish doesn't have a shade. Gwen Stefani doesn't have a shade. And you're not going to have one either. No more blending into the background."

"What sort of thing were you thinking then? I'm not going short or too brassy."

"A sleek, perfectly proportioned bob is what you need. Something that says you can't screw with me but you can take me to your grandma's and I'll still look good. You'll present as smart, sexy, and sophisticated all at the same time."

Kirin suppressed a grin at his assessment of the way her new look might work, but she shook her head. "I've always had long hair. I'm not going to change it now. Especially not for a bob. "

He sighed and tossed the magazine so it slid across the table in front of him. He fixed her with a hard-edged stare. "Okay, you can stop it now."

She tried to wriggle upright, but the movement made her sink lower. "Stop it?"

He said nothing for a moment, but seemed to take a deeper breath. "Yes, stop it. The road-blocking, the heel-digging, the pain-in-the-ass, pig-headed attitude you have every time we look at something new. I told you there are certain things we're going to do, and for each of them you're going to have to trust me. We have a photo shoot in a couple days, events to attend, maybe even a talk show appearance, and I'm not going to have you appear in any of them if things aren't right." He flicked his hand in the air as if she were a particularly irritating insect.

She chewed the inside of her cheek, surprised at his hard-edged tone but strangely satisfied she was getting under his skin. Perhaps there *was* a passionate heart beating inside that muscular chest, after all.

"It's clear from the way you immediately say no to all my suggestions that you don't trust me at all." He counted off on his fingers. "It's day three and we have no outfits chosen, no shoes that you like, you can't take instructions on how to stand, and you're fighting me on hair color. We're not making any progress." He fell back against the chair, his eyes flashing emerald and the slightest red showing in his cheeks. The shiny coat of control was slipping, and it made him even more handsome.

"I'm trying, Blake. I've come to each of the appointments you've asked me to, been picked up by anonymous drivers. I've scurried in through back doors like some sort of criminal. I'm being open to the options you're presenting, but I can't ignore my instincts. My own self-knowledge. My transformation has to be authentic to get my life back."

He clasped his hands together in front of him and the stare went from hard-edged to withering. And it was a serious turn on.

His dark eyebrows dipped, sending a delicious shiver down her spine. "There won't be any life back if there's no buy-in from you, Kirin. I understand you're used to being in control. I know you built this image for a reason, but as I said right from the very first day, if you want a quick turnaround, then you need to make changes that are proven to work. One of those is an up-to-date hair color."

"What I don't get…" She sank further into the couch until her knees were almost at ear height. "Is why you're so certain that this isn't all going to backfire? How can you be so sure that people are going to believe this new, sexily confident person is the real me?"

"Because it *is* the real you."

"You think you've got people so figured out, don't you?"

He grinned. "Not people. Just you. You're my sole focus right now, so yes, I think I've got your number."

Despite the fact that in so many ways his confidence in her was irritating, it sparked something deep inside. A need she hadn't felt in a very long time. Should she go along with it? Tell a big fat lie that it *was* the real her just to experience his reaction, or should she stop it here and now?

The thrill subsided. She had to work with this unbelievably attractive man for the next two weeks, avoid the sort of flattery that had caused this whole mess in the first place.

He scrubbed a hand across his chin, and she almost squeaked it was so sexy. His green-eyed stare became more sincere. "I wouldn't be pushing you on this spiced-up image if I didn't think you could handle it, Kirin. I know you have the confidence to carry this off, but I also know that if you let yourself relax just a little, you could really have fun with this. You don't have to believe it all, you just have to look like you do. Just relax."

"I am relaxed." She crossed her legs the other way.

"The hell you are. You worry all the time about yourself, rather than just going with your gut and letting things roll. Have a bit of fun with it all." He blinked lazily. "Have a bit of fun with me."

Watching him there in his teal blue shirt and tanned skin, his perfect jaw line and achingly handsome smile, she wanted to make a deeper connection. "You know what it's like? Having to worry all the time about how you're presenting yourself to people? I'm guessing you haven't wasted a second on it in your lifetime. I bet you've never had a pimple. Never had to wear a hat because it looked like things were nesting in your hair. Never had stomach cramps because you've spent the day sucking your belly in."

He raised an eyebrow, but she carried on. "I bet you've never once walked into a room and wanted to dissolve into the floorboards because you knew with stomach-churning certainty you'd worn the wrong thing."

He scoffed. "You don't have the monopoly on feeling uncomfortable. Of course I've experienced those things. It was my job. Modeling is all about presenting the image the client wants, reinventing your outward self at the snap of someone's fingers. I've worried plenty about whether I had good enough muscle definition, or if my hair was thinning..." He dipped his chin and grinned. "Which it isn't, by the way."

"But you're naturally . . . stunning. You know what to wear and how to wear it. I just can't do that."

He rolled his eyes skyward. "And that's another thing."

"What?"

"Stop running yourself down all the time. It's boring, and it's deeply unattractive."

"I don't run myself down."

"You do. You'll often say it as a joke, like your feet are too big or you have no sense of style, and it's a pain in the ass. As you've seen in the last month or so there are enough people willing to drag you down without you doing it, too."

Boy, there was a delicious pleasure in irritating him. "But I'm joking when I say those things."

He shook his head. "It's not funny, and it's not smart. Have you ever heard me do it?"

She thought for a second. He'd said very little about himself at all, and certainly nothing negative. This back-and-forth banter was the closest she'd come to feeling like she knew him. Not that he was always blowing his own trumpet, but he certainly presented himself in a good light. She ignored the question. "So you're becoming my shrink now?"

"If I have to be. When we get to media training—"

"Media training?!"

"We'll be looking at the way you present on TV and in print and that self-critical thing's going to be first to go. The first lesson's tomorrow, and I want you looking your best. Your public's not going to love your new style if you don't love it yourself. This is cold, hard business, Kirin. If you believe in what we're doing, then you're public's going to believe it too."

She was silent, but his stare remained.

"You can hate me all you like, but doing this is going to get you back the life you want. The life you worked so hard for."

She didn't hate him, and that was the problem. She could've sat looking at the touched-by-gods face of Blake Matthews, having him focus solely on her, all day long.

She chewed her bottom lip. "I don't hate you. I just wish you had even the tiniest idea what it's like to have your whole outward appearance criticized day in and day out."

He blew out a sharp breath as Colin, the hairdresser, appeared. She was glad they'd had this out. He needed to know that none of this was as easy for her as he thought it was. It was normal for a thirty-four-year-old woman to want to be accepted just the way she was—but that was something Blake would never do for her.

She smiled at Colin. Blake had been right. He was nothing like she'd imagined. He was dressed in business pants, a white shirt rolled to the sleeves, and a charcoal tie. "Nice to meet you, Kirin, I've been a fan for a long time."

"Thanks." She struggled to get out of the couch, and when Blake reached out a hand, she grabbed hold. Their eyes met, and he pulled her up and winked. She thought she might die from the zing that shot straight to her chest.

"My wife loves your oil rubs."

Oil rubs? She was still holding Blake's hand and her mind tumbled back to him being bare-chested, but this time she was rubbing him down with oil. Mentally slapping herself, she focused back on Colin.

Blake cleared his throat. "I've briefed Colin on what sort of look I'm after, and I'll leave you in his hands."

"You're leaving?" She hadn't expected him to go. Despite the disagreement right now, she still didn't feel comfortable about doing any of this on her own. Panic became a steel ball in her throat.

Blake smiled slowly. "I've got some things to set up for

tomorrow. I'll drop by your place later with the outfit you'll be wearing for media training. See you then."

Blake walked through the parking lot and cursed the stubborn woman he'd left behind in the salon. God, she was infuriating . . . and mesmerizing. He couldn't get her out of his head.

One minute she was strong and defiant, the next unsure of herself and questioning. At that moment of vulnerable indecision, when a little line formed between her brows, it made him want to drag her close and whisper that he'd get this right for her. She could trust him, always.

Yesterday's incident with Trent had played over in his mind and each time he was left with a feeling deep in his chest that he wanted to be there for Kirin, do whatever he could to protect her.

He wanted to know more of her, too. The sexy side that she didn't even know she possessed. The way she ran her tongue over her lips when she was nervous, the way she played with the thin gold chain around her neck. And the way she believed so much in her business that she'd stand up to him when he challenged her held him fascinated.

Just what sort of lingerie did she wear? What sort of fantasies did she have in the privacy of her own home?

What he'd really like to do was uncover a little of that secret side of Kirin tonight. Chip away at the unbelievably hard shell she surrounded herself with and get to know the real Kirin Hart. And that had nothing at all to do with business.

He swallowed and shook the memories of her off. She might have him fascinated, but he still had a job to do.

He was due to give a report to one of the Dent and Douglas partners tomorrow about what progress he'd made with Kirin, and so far he had nothing.

Never had he worked with someone so clueless about fashion and presentation. Even some of the corporate men he styled knew about the difference between a well-cut suit and a cheap one. Kirin not only had no knowledge of what she should wear and how she should present herself, but she had no interest in learning, either.

If he didn't have something dramatic to report soon, the board of directors at Dent and Douglas would lose patience. And then they wouldn't sell. D and D would be the shining jewel in his image business crown. He had to work harder with Kirin.

He grinned as he imagined what she'd be like tomorrow, eyes sparkling as she attempted to run the media training, her sweet lips pursing as she argued with him about which outfit she'd be wearing and how she'd be presented.

His phone rang, and the light on the screen showed his brother's number. What the hell did he want? He hadn't spoken to Bryn in months and didn't feel like getting into anything with him now, but there'd been a couple of messages from him at the office and Blake hadn't gotten around to calling him back. It could be about their father. The old man hadn't been well for some time and what if... He pressed talk. "Hey."

"You're a hard man to track down."

"Busy. You know." He reached into his pocket for his keys and stabbed the unlock button. "I'm sure you're in the same boat. How's the doctor business?"

There was a pause. "The doctor business is great. How's the dress-up business?"

Even though he'd been the one to ask the question, and

even though he teased his brother about the importance of his job whenever they spoke, it cut deep every time Bryn and his parents made fun of him. Every. Single. Time.

"You need to come home."

"What for?"

"We need to get Mom and Dad sold up. They can't cope with living on the farm anymore. I've found a retirement home for them in Salem and I need you to come help me persuade them to move."

Blake opened the car door and slid into the seat. "I can't come right now. Maybe in a couple weeks when I've sorted this major project."

A snort sounded down the line. "Oh, don't tell me. Some model needs advice on how to wear her hair a little longer." Bryn's voice had changed from cultivated charm to sarcastic in a second. "No, wait, it's probably an advertisement for silicone implants that you're fronting."

Blake squeezed the keys in his hands until the sharp edge of one dug into his palm. Stay calm. Prove him wrong.

"I'm busy, Bryn, and no I'm not saving the world, one patient at a time, like you are, but I've put a hell of a lot of time and energy into my business and it's about to pay off. I can't go to Oregon right now."

There was silence for a minute. "It's nothing less than I'd expect. When you've finished styling the stars, maybe you can take a moment or two to think about some real people with *real* problems." The phone went dead, and he swore under his breath.

He thumped the steering wheel. Damn Bryn. Every time he spoke with his brother, the same childish need to justify his life and his business reared up inside him. Being an image consultant wasn't so far removed from his brother's job as a micro-surgeon. They were both in the business of changing the way people looked, but, apparently, one job was so much more meaningful than the other.

He *would* go back to Oregon, just as soon as he'd made some decent progress with Kirin. The thought of spending more time with her put the smile back on his face and he sat straighter in his seat. So much would change in his life when he'd secured D and D, not the least of which would prove to his family that he was worth more than what he saw in the mirror. Kirin was the key.

"Oh. My. God." Kirin leaned forward in the chair, hardly able to believe the stylish woman staring back at her from the mirror. Gone was the hair she'd worn halfway down her back since she was fourteen. Gone was the bleached and straight look she'd loved since she first saw the surfer boys in California. Replacing it was a layered, sophisticated cut—not the bob Blake had wanted—that brushed her shoulders. She moved her head just a little and a curtain of hair swung to and fro.

Carefully, she reached up and smoothed her palm down the length. "You call this a sexy cut?" She'd imagined something far more wild, far more like what her mother would wear, with the fringe a little too long, the color a little too bright.

"Take a look at the back." Colin held the mirror up, and she ran her hand down the honey colored length. "Blake's not going to be happy it's not a bob, but I think you were right, it's a perfect look for you."

"Do you style for a lot of his clients?" She turned her head this way and that.

"I was the personal stylist to his girlfriend, Ellen, for years and when they broke up, we stayed in touch."

"Oh." A million questions raced through her head, but only one left her mouth. "Was she stunning?"

"Meh." Colin shrugged a shoulder. "Maybe on the outside, but on the inside she was as frozen as the polar ice caps."

Kirin found her voice as a whisper. "Did she break his heart?"

Colin snorted. "If you want my opinion—and since I'm now your stylist, you'll get it whether you want it or not—Blake likes the drama of being with someone he's never really going to get close to. It suits his controlling nature and ensures he'll never have to be vulnerable."

"That sounds a little harsh."

"Oh, you get that with the twenty-somethings." He unclipped the plastic cape from her shoulders and she stood. "People like you and I know what life's about. It's all downhill after thirty and we have to take a trolley to the beauty store to get all our products, but someone like Blake can rest on his laurels and play the hunk card for plenty of years yet. There'll be a few hearts kicked to the curb before he's finished."

She stared into the mirrored wall while Colin continued to chat and make arrangements for her next appointment. Both Lucy and Colin had suggested Blake was a lady-killer, a ruthless player who'd left a trail of broken hearts in his wake. And instead of that turning her off him and warning her to keep her distance, she was shocked to discover it excited her in a way she hadn't been excited in a very long time.

But she knew any sort of personal connection with Blake was completely out of the question. He was a younger man, her employee really, and there was no way on God's good earth that she would feed any of the lies and slander that had swirled around her for months.

Her throat dried. A private and primal part of her wanted to get as close to Blake Matthews as any woman could, and she had to keep that to herself for ten whole days.

6

___

*I*t was almost nine when Kirin answered Blake's knock at her door later that evening. He often liked to signal to his clients that they were his top priority, but hand delivering the outfit for Kirin's media training tomorrow was more than that. He wanted to be clear that rejecting this one wasn't an option. She'd wear what he said she'd wear this time or be damned. He'd pussyfooted around long enough.

Dudley's bass notes greeted him as he set foot inside. He was sitting at the end of the hallway like some ancient gargoyle, and Blake could've sworn the dog was giving him the stink eye.

"I'm just making something to eat," Kirin said as he followed her toward the kitchen. Rich, buttery smells were coming from the back of the house, and his stomach grumbled in response.

"What kind of cut do you call that?" He tried to keep his eyes on her hair but was getting distracted by the sway of her hips in her tight tan skirt as she walked ahead of him.

"I had a little disagreement with Colin," she said as they reached the kitchen.

"You mean you persuaded him to cut your hair the way *you* wanted. No one does that."

She threw a sparkling smile over her shoulder. "I do. Here, I'll take that." She reached for the suit bag he was holding and for the first time he was given the full impact of her new look. Her whole face lit up. The new light honey color of her hair contrasted with the deep brown of her eyes, and the style framed her face perfectly. He couldn't have chosen better himself.

She blinked, then frowned, and he realized he'd been staring. Clearing his throat, he passed her the garment bag. "You'll wear this for the first media training session tomorrow. You won't need me there, but I'll have a driver pick you up and drop you back."

"Okay, I hope I like it."

"Liking's irrelevant. I've put the instant camera in so you can take some self-timer shots wearing this different ways. And no sabotaging my plans like you did with the hair."

She bit her lip and shot him a devious look from beneath her lashes. God, she was hot when she was being defiant.

"I know you like it." She gave her head an overly dramatic toss. "It's going to be easy to style, and it's long enough that I can still put it up in an alligator clip, but don't tell Lucy."

He chuckled as she laid the bag across a chair. It took some sort of woman to be ballsy and funny at the same time.

"Hungry?" she asked. "I had a craving for a three cheese gnocchi and salad. It won't take a minute."

He had no clue what a three cheese gnocchi was, but he

wouldn't stay. It'd be an early start tomorrow, and he wanted to fit in a run at dawn. "No, thanks. I'll see you Saturday after the photo shoot at my apartment. A weekend shoot in a private location fits with us keeping things under the radar, but it'll just be you and Alex, the photographer, I'm afraid. I'm meeting with a friend who can help us with a new TV launch for you, so I'll come by after that. I'll get a selection of outfits to you tomorrow, and Alex will meet you at the apartment."

Standing still, she narrowed her eyes at him. "What have you eaten today?" She'd completely ignored what he'd just said.

"Sorry?"

"Food. What have you had today?"

What had he eaten? It took a few seconds to remember. "A protein shake after my run this morning, half a burger at lunch, and a cookie from a gas station after I left you with Colin."

"I don't know how you exist." She moved behind the counter and began checking a pan on the stove. "I bet you don't even know what was in the burger."

"Sure I do." He speared his fingers through his hair and looked back at the front door he should leave through, then back to her at the stove. There was something about the homeliness of this place, the comforting cooking smells, Dudley lounging on his luxurious cushion, and the vision of Kirin in her kitchen that made it hard to leave. "There was some meat and some green stuff."

He looked up to see her rolling her eyes. "Nutrition, that's what your body needs. Fresh food that's been cooked with love, not stuff you grab on the run. When was the last time someone cooked for you?"

He shrugged. "Last week when I ate at the little Italian place underneath my apartment."

She laughed. "I'm surprised you can do all that running when you eat so badly." She assembled a knife, chopping board, and the makings of a salad. "You're staying for dinner, and I won't take no for an answer."

He watched as she bent her head, and the strangest feeling overtook him. When was the last time someone had shown such basic concern for him? Cared about what and when he'd eaten? It chilled him to realize he couldn't remember.

He strolled to her display shelf, the warmth of her interest settling on him. He bent down and looked at the enormous collection of salt and pepper shakers "I run so I *can* eat badly. When did you start collecting these?"

She threw a look to where he was standing and resumed cooking. "My mother gave me my very first pair—the couple from American Gothic—when I left Iowa, to remind me of where I came from."

"Which are your favorite?"

She began slicing something at the counter. "See the Laurel and Hardy ones? They were my grandmother's. I can't help smiling when I look at them. I love the idea of couples who complement each other like salt and pepper. I had Scarlett and Rhett from Gone with the Wind but someone knocked Rhett's head off and I couldn't bear to have Scarlett sitting there on her own."

For a fleeting moment, Blake thought of his apartment. There were no shelves with knick-knacks there. Rented furniture, a suitcase full of clothes, but if he were honest, it wasn't so different from his place back in New York. He'd hired a decorating company to furnish his Manhattan apartment, but he spent so little time there he never cooked or entertained.

Kirin was such a mish-mash. Her poor background and then her fame, the plain way she presented herself, her quirky side with the salt and pepper shakers, and her sense of humor after all that had happened.

"Tell me about your hobbies?" She looked up from where she was chopping at the counter and gave him a toe-curling smile.

"Hobbies? No hobbies. Too busy."

"You must have something. No one can live on work alone. Tell me about the running. You must enjoy that."

"I started running to help maintain my weight when I was modeling, and it's become part of my normal routine. No one wants an out of shape image consultant."

She tilted her head as she stopped chopping. "Don't you get sick of it all?"

"The running?"

"The image industry. The models and the fashion. It's so subjective, isn't it? About what looks good and what doesn't?"

"I think most people know what looks stylish." He picked up a Batman shaker, then remembered her gray leggings from yesterday and considered revising that statement. "And anyone who tells you they don't judge a person by how they look is a bare-faced liar."

She reached for something on a high shelf and shook it into the bowl. "But focusing so much on looks is so empty, so finite. Doesn't that just depress you sometimes?" She was sounding just like Bryn, and the familiar defensive chill crawled up his spine.

"Of course not. It's my business. I earned my first million

because of my looks and my next learning how to enhance the looks of others. It's not finite for me."

"How long have you been with Dent and Douglas?"

He'd been expecting this question, so his answer came easily. "Not long. They're San Francisco's most prestigious PR firm so I feel very privileged to be associated with them."

She made a small sound.

"What?"

Her eyes crinkled at the corners. "I just don't see you as an employee."

He straightened. Her ability to sum him up so accurately spooked him and held him fascinated. "Why's that?"

"Oh, I don't know." A small smile curved her mouth. "You don't seem like you'd be able to take instructions very well."

He roared with laughter. "Is that right?"

"You seem more like someone who'd want to run the company." She called to Dudley and put what looked like a bowl of chopped steak on the floor.

She could be as insightful as she liked, but he wouldn't tell her the truth just yet. He wanted her to trust what he was doing for her. Hell, he wanted her to trust *him*. Telling her that his whole future depended on the success of her transformation could make her run for the hills. Or doubt his advice. He didn't want her thinking his strategy was based solely on his own ends.

"Tell me what really happened with Trent Bray." He came closer to watch her cook. Just like the very first time he saw her, he was mesmerized by every movement—from the way she sprinkled salt into a pot of boiling water to the way she checked the freshness of the vegetables. There was a confidence in her that he hadn't seen a lot of lately, and it was very sexy.

She kept slicing a tomato in swift, clean strokes, but even from where he stood he could hear the increased pressure as the knife hit the wood of the chopping board, see her grip on the black handle grow tighter.

"I've told you what happened." She stopped and brushed the back of her hand across her forehead and then resumed the cutting without looking up. "He started to flirt with me. It began as a bit of banter to begin with. He did it in such an insidious way I hardly even noticed." She paused. "Then he'd bring me coffee and stay longer in my office than was necessary. He'd wait until I was ready to go home, then walk with me to the parking lot. I was too naïve to realize what he was doing and by the time he made a pass it was all too late." Concentrating hard on what she was doing, she lifted the chopping board and scraped the bright red tomatoes into the salad bowl.

Blake moved to the side of the counter, the Batman salt shaker still in his hand. "And you then told him to get the hell away from you, and that's when he took offense." She turned her back on him, looking for something.

"That's what happened, isn't it, Kirin? You told the jerk to keep away, and he took offense?"

Suddenly she stopped what she was doing and stood frozen on the spot.

"Kirin?" She didn't move, and he realized he was holding a breath, waiting for her answer. He took a step toward her. "God, he didn't attack you, did he? Didn't assault you?" His fingers curled tight around the shaker. If that bastard had forced himself on her . . . someone so caring and open and honest.

She dragged in a breath and turned, then took a step back so she was pressed into the countertop. Her face was impassive, mouth quivering slightly at one corner. "He called me a frigid bitch."

"Oh, sweetheart...."

"He said I was so hard and probably so dried up that he wouldn't have been able to get close enough to me, anyway."

Blake stepped closer, but she held up both hands, palms outward, and dropped her head for a second before she looked him in the face again. "He said everyone knew I'd only slept with one man in my life so no wonder I didn't know what to do when someone made a move on me."

"What a prick."

She shook her head. "He was right. Joe was the first man I made love to, and he was also the last."

Blake let out a low whistle.

"When Trent made the allegation that I'd made a pass at him at a Christmas party I was so shocked that I wasn't sure I hadn't done something wrong. *Had* I stood too close? Touched his arm for too long?"

The confusion on her face and the hesitation in her voice caused his chest to constrict, and he burned to take all the pain away for her. Be the one who'd fight for her. "Did he make the allegation to other people?"

"He went to my HR manager, and she reported it to my board. It was humiliating, but I'd thought we'd resolved it. When he applied for a promotion a couple months later and didn't get it, he said the harassment had continued and that I'd sidestepped him for the job because he refused to sleep with me. That's when my lawyer advised an out of court settlement to make it go away."

Blake put the ornament on the counter beside her and touched her arm. The soft skin warmed his hand, and he curled his fingers to feel more of her. "You didn't believe that jerk? You didn't think you were that cold, hard woman he said you were. Or that you'd treated him badly."

Of course she did. It was written in the lines by her mouth and the uncertain look in her eye. And it made him want to pull her close and whisper how wrong she was. "I don't know."

"Kirin, you can't believe him. From the very first day I saw you I was awed by your self-confidence, your drive to put your business back on the right track. That's what blew me away about you. And I bet those were the things Bray wished he'd had for himself."

"I haven't had sex in five years." Her words were a whisper.

Had he heard her right? He shook his head. "You don't have to tell me all this. I shouldn't have asked."

"No, I think you need to understand, because it's impacting on your work here."

He left his hand on her arm and stroked the underside with his thumb while she continued.

"Joe and I grew apart and didn't have a sex life for years. And the couple of guys I dated after he died only wanted to be seen with me to advance their own careers. When all this happened with Trent, I wondered if maybe he was right. Maybe I am a frigid bitch. I think that's why I can't do all this sexing up stuff." She hooked him with her liquid caramel eyes, and he dragged his thumb across the smooth skin at her wrist.

"I'll never believe you're not a sensual woman. Not in a million years."

For an endless second she looked at him and the saucepan lid chattering on the stove matched the beat, hard and heavy, in his chest. He stepped forward and cupped her cheek in his palm. "You're beautiful, Kirin. You're desirable to any man. Don't doubt that for a second. A lot of what you and I are doing together is finding the closed part of you, bringing it out in the open so you're confident in the whole of yourself. So your fans can see the real you."

He dipped his face closer, and the air between them sparked. Nothing mattered more right now than being as close to her as he could get. "We can find it together." Before he had another thought, his mouth was against hers. He slid his tongue between her lips, and the small sound she made in the back of her throat fired him hotter. He dragged her close and devoured the honey-sweet mouth he'd been watching and wanting.

Her fingers threaded up his neck and she pulled him towards her until they were chest to chest, jammed against the countertop. He deepened the kiss, the warm scent of freshly cut tomatoes and citrus shampoo causing it to become a feast.

In a dance of tongue and lip, his mind fogged, his only focus the way his skin heated under hers, his pulse rushing. Wanting more of her, he dragged himself from her lips, then kissed a line from that sweet, lush mouth down her delicate jaw. He pushed back the drape of hair and nuzzled the milky skin of her neck. The flutter of her pulse against his lips fired him.

"Mmmm, Blake, hang on." She whispered as she moved her hands to his chest, "We shouldn't do this. We can't possibly do this."

He looked into her face and the flush on her skin and the spark in her eyes told him her indecision wasn't matching what was running through her blood.

"We can do whatever you want." He moved his face close again and kissed the delicate lobe of her ear. "It's just a kiss..."

"You're gorgeous." She moaned as she pushed him back and gazed into his face. "I can hardly take my eyes off you when we're together. It's like having to look at a black forest gateau every morning when I'm on a diet. But you know this is impossible as much as I do."

He smiled. He'd found her watching him in the last few days, saw the way the color rushed to her face when he'd caught her. He'd been around women long enough to know when they were attracted to him, and there was no doubt in his mind about Kirin. And he wanted her just as much.

"Okay." He let his hands drop by his sides. "If that's what you want, but I could've sworn you enjoyed that kiss."

She wet her lips. "Of course I did, but it was a sympathy kiss after what I told you about Trent. I don't need your sympathy."

Blake thought about the pressure in his jeans right now, the way his chest had thumped when her pulse skipped beneath his fingers. "There were a whole lot of reasons why I kissed you just now. Sympathy didn't figure."

"It couldn't work." She moved her eyes from his face and back again. "Could it?" Her tone had slipped between a statement and a question. "My business means way more to me than a relationship—you said yourself I can't be dating anyone right now—and I thought you understood that."

He smiled slowly. "Who said anything about a relationship?"

Kirin willed her heart to stop sprinting and her knees to keep her steady.

Blake kissing her was a figment of the dreams that made her toss and turn at night, not something she ever expected in reality. And it was the way he'd kissed her—with hungry, open-mouthed desire—that had every cell in her body screaming to let it happen again. The fact she was standing here now with his heat still pulsing on her lips and his broad chest only a touch away was enough to make every thought in her head scramble.

I haven't had sex for five years. What in all hell had she been thinking telling him that? What else could the poor, honorable guy do but give her a kiss to make her feel better?

It might've been the most perfect kiss she could've imagined, but she'd experienced the flattery and attention of a younger man before and look where that had gotten her.

"Well, if it wasn't a relationship, then it would be shallow, meaningless sex, wouldn't it?" she said.

"I guess it would." Blake lifted a finger and ran it slowly from her shoulder to her elbow, and her skin flamed. His voice was as sinfully rich as her secret caramel sauce recipe, and she almost melted on the spot. "But if we both knew what it was going in, then there wouldn't be a problem. Making love always means something. Maybe it's the key we've been looking for. The way to help you find your authentic sexy self."

A champagne fizz flowed through her veins with the way he was stroking her. What woman wouldn't kill to be seduced by Blake Matthews, in her own kitchen, with three cheese gnocchi to follow? But she hadn't gotten where she was in the world by making rash and libido-fueled decisions.

She stilled. In truth, she'd never once made a rash, libido-filled decision. And where, in fact, was she in the world right now? Still at rock bottom.

She looked into Blake's confident face, and something shifted inside her. What if he was right and this was exactly what she needed? To break the shackles of her loveless marriage with Joe, the feelings of shame and confusion with Trent? Maybe a short, sexy fling with a young, carefree guy like Blake could help her find the elusive sexy side that he seemed so certain she had hidden inside her.

She took a steadying breath. No, it was madness.

Tucking a piece of stray hair behind her ear, she willed her voice steady. "It would destroy everything if we were found out. My reputation as a cougar would be cemented, and you wouldn't have succeeded in changing my image. Disaster for both of us."

"True," he said. "But we've perfected the art of stealth already, and we're only talking another ten days. I think we could do it. If we had agreed boundaries and a clear objective." His eyes smoldered. "We'd both have plenty to gain."

She reached across the counter and turned off the saucepan. This felt like a business discussion. A sexy, secret business discussion that both horrified and thrilled her.

She schooled her voice into a tone that was a whole lot more definite than she felt. "As much as I'd love to take you up on your offer, I think there's too much at stake. I propose that for the remainder of our two weeks we acknowledge our attraction to each other but that we put our own goals ahead of that."

He just smiled, a look so challenging and so naughty her body flamed.

She tossed her head. "No more discussions about lingerie or my sex life, or the things we could get up to together. From now on we focus on business and nothing more."

He folded his arms across his chest, his grin even sexier than before. "If you think you can stick to that. Not sure I can."

She turned back to the gnocchi before she could change her mind.

Blake walked from his car to Kirin's gate the next afternoon, a pile of garment covers slung across his arm. He'd made a dignified exit, full of Kirin's unbelievably good gnocchi, last night. There'd only been conversations about the food and her media training after the aborted kiss, though.

But he hadn't stopped thinking about it. About the hunger he'd sensed in her, the flame that had ignited when he'd slipped his tongue between her lips, and he knew she'd felt something. The way her eyes grew wide and sparkled wasn't the only giveaway.

It was lucky he'd organized for her to take the first media training on her own today. It would give him a chance to consider his next move.

When he'd learned she hadn't made love in five years, that her lack of sexual confidence wasn't because she wasn't interested, but through a lack of an intimate relationship, something new had stirred inside him. It was wrong that a woman so unique, so interesting, and beautiful was so inexperienced in making love.

He'd sent her a text saying he'd drop the clothes by this evening, but she'd said Lucy was bringing her sister Pippa by to give her some makeup tips. She told him where her spare key was and asked him to do it during the day.

When he reached the gate, he stopped. A woman was knocking on her front door, a woman in very tight, black skinny jeans and a large white sweater. Her faded blonde hair was piled on her head with a neon pink hair thing, a large bag slung over her thin shoulder.

Maybe the cleaner. And it looked like she'd lost her keys. She bent down to a large ceramic frog—the place Kirin had told him he'd find the key—and retrieved something from beneath it. She then stood and placed a key in the door.

He could go away and come back later, or he could leave the clothes inside as he'd told Kirin he would. The chance to go inside her peaceful home one more time won out. If he couldn't spend the day with her, then stepping foot inside a place that carried the same scent of spring flowers he caught whenever she walked by would do 'til he could see her again. He closed the gate behind him and walked up the path and through the front door. The sound of out-of-tune humming was coming from the kitchen, and as much as he'd have liked to leave the clothes and go, it was only polite to let the woman know he was here.

He cleared his throat at the doorway to the kitchen, and she let out a high-pitched squeal. "Oh, Lord save me!" Her hand slammed against her generous chest. "Who in all hell are you? And why did you creep up on me like that? I almost dropped these beautiful shakers."

Dudley barked in the corner like the Hound of the Baskervilles, and Blake was frozen to the spot, staring at Kirin's visitor. The caramel eyes beneath long lashes, the delicate jawline, and milky skin—there was no mistaking Kirin's mother. She must only be in her early fifties, but it was hard to tell exactly. She dressed like someone half her age, the dark kohl around her eyes making her look night-club-ready.

"Shut up, Dudley!" They both shouted at once and Dudley stopped mid-bark, a long string of drool dripping from his mouth as he lay back down on his cushion.

"I'm sorry," he said. "I'm dropping something off for Kirin, and since you're here I thought I'd bring it in."

The woman shrugged and kept on taking newspaper out of a cardboard box. "Well, it's nice to see you, Sugar. I'm Kirin's momma, Candice. But you can call me Candi. Are you a friend of hers? I forgot my key but luckily I remembered she keeps one under the toad on her front step." She cooed to Dudley, and he waddled over to have his ears rubbed.

Blake looked over to the spot where he'd dragged Kirin into his arms last night. "Something like that. More of a business acquaintance."

She pulled a porcelain figure of what looked like Prince Charles out of the box and placed it carefully with the rest of Kirin's salt and pepper collection. "I got these two beauties from the thrift store near where I do my painting. Aren't they darling? I was hoping Kirin would be here so I could give them to her in person but looks like she's out."

"They are *something*," he said. "I'm Blake Matthews."

"Oh, are you the guy giving her the makeover?" Her eyes rounded, and she pursed her coral pink lips together. "She's told me all about what you're doing, and all I can say is how sorry I am that you're the one who drew the short straw."

He drew closer. "Why's that?"

"Because I don't like your chances. Kirin's a sweetheart, but she's a controlling sweetheart." She drew a Princess Diana shaker from the other box and set it beside Charles and gave it a pat. It was then he noticed her fingernails. They were so long they almost curved, and they were painted brilliant red.

"She's never had much of an in how she presents herself." She began to remove the white sweater. "Never interested in clothes or make-up. I'm going to make a pot of tea. Do you want a cup? We can wait for Kirin. I want to see her face when I show her the new shakers."

"No thanks to the tea." Blake watched her move toward the kitchen. "And Kirin might be a while, she's doing some media training today."

Now the sweater was gone, he saw she had paired a corset thing with purple velvet and dark green ribbons with the black jeans. It wouldn't have looked out of place on an alternative type of kid in college, but on Candi it looked odd.

Maybe Kirin's resistance to wearing something "sexier" came in part from her mom's dress sense. Kirin had mentioned something about hating the way her mom was treated in her waitressing job.

"So you think what we're doing with Kirin's look is working?" He leaned against the counter.

"I'm surprised you've managed to get her to do anything at all. She can be one stubborn woman, my Kirin, and although it's helped her success, it's also helped get her in a whole lotta trouble."

He leaned closer. "What do you mean?"

Candi put the kettle on the stove. "Kirin's never learned how to use her feminine wiles to get what she wants. She's too practical, too much like a man in the way she approaches things. I've always told her that her life could be a hell of a lot easier if she'd learn how to be softer. She tried on a pink top you'd given her the other day, and she looked stunning."

"She hated that top." He grinned, remembering the fight they'd had about whether it suited her or not.

"You must've persuaded her to wear it, though. I hope she listens to you more often, or she's gonna lose everything she worked for. Not having a man has created all this furor for her. While she had Joe, she was looked after and protected. Now she's all out on a limb for people to take potshots at her. Like that guy with the sex tape. Kirin wouldn't know what a sex tape was, let alone what to do on one. I hope she's paid you some attention while you've been looking after her."

She threw him a pointed look, and he cleared his throat. "I think Kirin's doing just fine without a man. She's confident. She knows exactly what she wants."

"And she's desperately unhappy. Don't let that control freak persona fool you, Blake. Kirin can't operate properly without a commanding man around." She winked. "Maybe you can help her."

He suppressed his shock. "That's not the sort of relationship we have. As soon as our project's over we'll be going our separate ways."

Candi tilted her head and smiled. "That's what you say now, but wait until she's laid one of her guilt trips on you. Then we'll see who's the one in control."

"I don't know what you mean."

"Kirin has a particular talent for making people feel as though they've screwed things up for her. Oh, I know she loves me and we have a laugh together, but she blames me for some of the hang-ups she's had in her life. And she blamed Joe, too. You need to watch her."

"I'm sure I'll be fine."

"Hmm, maybe you will be." Candi seemed to re-evaluate him. "Maybe you can hold a mirror up so she can see that it's not always others who she needs to blame. If you can do that and change the way she presents herself, you'll be worth all the money she's paying you."

Kirin: Okay, girls I need your advice on what to do about Doomed Blake.

Gwin: Of course. Is BB being too bossy? Telling you what side to butter your toast on.

Kirin: If it were only that simple…

Ellie: We're always here for you K. What's been happening?

Kirin stared at the computer screen. Should she really open up to them about her deepest, most conflicted thoughts? It would do damage to both her *and* Blake if her real feelings were made public. And yet, Ellie and Gwin didn't know who she was. They must have guessed she was hiding something when she'd only given them an initial. But they'd been nothing but supportive until now.

To them, she was together and normal.

Kirin: I think I should fire Blake.

Gwin: Because . . . ? You said that one of your goals was NOT to fire the next image consultant. What's going wrong with him?

Kirin: I did say that, didn't I? Well, it's not so much that he's doing anything wrong. In fact, he seems to have put his whole life on hold to sort me out.

Ellie: Has BB been too blunt? Telling you to change things about yourself that you don't agree with? I'd have a hard time with a guy telling me to change anything about myself, but I know you need his help for your business.

Kirin: No, not too blunt. He says he believes there's a sexy, hidden part of me that we can uncover. But the trouble is, the sexy secret part thinks he's hot and desirable and I find I can't concentrate on anything when he's around.

Gwin: And that's not good because of the allegations against you?

Kirin: Exactly. Giving in to those feelings would be like dropping dynamite on a campfire. Do you think I should fire him?

Ellie: Well, you *are* consenting adults. It's not like you'd really be breaking any rules if something happened between you. You 're not in a power situation and he's not really an employee.

Kirin: That's true.

Gwin: And I'm going to go out on a limb and say I've noticed a difference in you since he's been around. I know we've only chatted a few times, but there's been a lightness in you since you've been working with BB.

Ellie: And isn't part of this whole deal with him about finding the real you? Maybe getting *hawt* and heavy with BB will help that process.

Kirin: The logical and controlled part of myself says to run as far away from this as possible, but the tiny little part that I can feel unfurling inside myself says that spending time with him is doing me good.

Gwin: One important consideration is—do you trust him? It sounds to me like a lot of the men in your life haven't been trustworthy.

Kirin: That's part of why I'm hesitating. I clearly haven't had a good radar for deceitful guys in the past, so why should I trust Blake, or trust my belief in him now.

Ellie: That is a big consideration.

Gwin: Has he told you much about himself?

Kirin: Not really. He always wants to be focused on me which is nice, but maybe I do need to find out a bit more about him.

Gwin: That would be the litmus test for me. If he can be open about who he is and you feel you can trust him then why not stay working together?

They carried on chatting about the challenges Ellie was facing in her project and the exciting plans Gwin had for her move to the city, and all the while a peaceful calm came over Kirin. Blake was good for her. They were making progress, and she was starting to feel so differently about herself. Now she just needed him to open up a little more and then she'd be truly happy about where this time with him was heading.

7
———

*B*lake let himself into his apartment building the next afternoon and took the elevator to the penthouse suite.

There was a lightness in his gut that could've been from only having had a protein shake today, but it was probably more about the anticipation of seeing Kirin again. Despite it being almost forty-eight hours since they were together, he could still taste the sweet heat of her mouth on his, feel her lush curves beneath his fingers.

Although she'd rejected finding her sensual side through making love with him for now, it wouldn't be the last time she'd be in his arms. He'd seen a different side of Kirin lately, a softer, more vulnerable side, and he couldn't stop thinking about her. She'd been through so much, and yet she still held on to what she believed in.

It was strange to think of her in his living room when they'd never been here together. She'd sent a text thanking him for the outfits last night. As she hadn't mentioned her mother, he presumed she hadn't caught up with Candi about their unexpected meeting.

When he stepped from the elevator, the photographer was picking up the last of his equipment.

"Thanks, Alex," he said with a nod. "I owe you."

"No problem. After you got me that job with Time, I'm in your debt for life." He dropped his voice. "Although if I'm going to go to the ends of the Earth for you it'd be good if you found someone less difficult to photograph." Alex nodded in the direction of Kirin who was loudly opening and shutting cupboards in the kitchen.

"Difficult?" Blake asked.

"Difficult I can cope with." Alex slung a bag over his shoulder. "Uncomfortable in front of the camera and with severe confidence issues. I'll be lucky if I have ten decent shots." He patted his camera case and headed toward the elevator. "Good luck. I get the feeling she's hungry and might devour the first moving thing she sees."

Blake shrugged out of his jacket, threw it on the couch, and strolled into the kitchen. "How'd it go?"

Dressed in an aqua sheath top and skirt which hugged every delicious curve of her, Kirin's new, lighter blond hair curled around her face and made her eyes shine. A strand of creamy pearls lay at her throat, and she fingered them as she spoke. "It was a long day. Harder than I imagined it would be. I thought I'd learned enough from you in the last few days, but I'm not sure I got it right." Anxious eyes held his.

Trying to distract himself from the tantalizing shape of her, he moved to the refrigerator, opened it, and peered in. "Trust me. You got it very right. I'd have been here if I could, but I got caught up talking with some studio execs about a new TV show that I think you'll be pleased with." Instead of the regular sight of protein bars and beer in the fridge, it was filled with green stuff and various colorful jars. "Oh, and I met your mother."

"My mother?" He turned back to see her face drop.

"I dropped by to leave the outfits at your house yesterday, and she was there. She's not what I expected."

"What did you expect?"

"Someone a lot more . . . conservative."

"You mean someone dressed more like a Sunday school teacher than one on the hunt."

He didn't reply until she looked at him again. "That's not what I meant."

"It's what most people think. They always have." There was a hard edge to her voice that he hadn't heard before, and he felt the pain of the relationship with her mom as his own.

"You don't like the way your mom dresses?"

"No, I don't, and I'm betting you don't either."

He shrugged. "It's not a very sophisticated look, but she seems to be having fun with it."

Kirin sighed. "She's not having fun, she's using it to try and snare herself another man. My mother's never been happy on her own. She thinks a woman without a man is a failure, that she needs protection and to be told what to do." She opened, then closed a cupboard. "The only attention she's ever valued was from men who wanted her to look more like a hooker than a waitress or a mother."

Blake nodded. Another little piece to the puzzle that was Kirin Hart slotted in to place. Her mother had used a sexy image to attract men, and Kirin had railed against it.

Given the look on her face and the way she was opening and shutting cupboard doors, he figured it was a good place to end the subject. "So, you found today difficult?"

"I did, but I guess it'll get easier," she said. "It's not so simple trying to work out which necklace goes with which dress. Whether to look sultry or sassy. Or even how to stand in the photos." She lifted an eyebrow. "I have a whole new level of respect for you."

"I'm sure you did a great job." He pulled out a beer and twisted the cap. "But I think you gave Alex a run for his money."

She sighed. "I did take my frustrations out on him a little. I'll apologize. He was fantastic and taught me a lot, too."

He nodded to the bottle. "You want a drink?"

"No, thanks." She looked around the kitchen and grinned. "I'm going to make pie."

"Pie? Now? I don't even know if that oven works."

She laughed, and he remembered her breath on his face, the way her lips had parted as he'd drawn her to him. There was no way he could carry on working this closely without making that happen again, and he would, at the first opportunity. He wanted to get as close to Kirin as any person could, but a flame of guilt licked at him. He still hadn't told her about the stakes involved in her makeover, or what they could lose if it didn't work out—for the company or between them.

"I've been standing in front of a camera for four hours, and I'm starving. I feel like pie."

"I'll find a deli and buy you one."

She threw him a disbelieving look and opened another cupboard. "Commercially made pies are mostly fillers. Very little substance and rendered fat in the pastry. I'm making a spinach and cheese pie from scratch. I told Alex I needed a lunch break and went out and bought all the ingredients, but I just assumed there'd be a pie plate to cook it in."

He took a swig from the bottle. "Can I watch?"

She turned to face him and chuckled. "Of course you can. Once I've changed out of this dress. I'm exhausted from holding my back straight and my tummy in. When I first heard about your job, I imagined lots of swanning about, but I can see how hard you must've worked as a model, and now."

He swallowed a mouthful of beer and noted her gaze moving to his throat. "I wish everyone had that insight."

"What do you mean?"

He frowned, the familiar dark cloud descending as he thought about the way his family reacted to his choice of profession.

"My family," he said. "They still believe I spend my days lounging in a director's chair telling people what shade of eye shadow to wear."

She looked puzzled. "They don't value what you do?"

He snorted. "Not many people do. In fact, you're the first person in a long time who's said anything positive. Not that it really matters to me, but I know the hard work people have to put in to change themselves and their image. I wouldn't be doing any of this if I didn't believe there was some worth both on a business level and a personal level. I wish more people were like you and could understand that there's a whole balance that needs to come into play." She nodded slowly, and it spurred him on. She did understand him. Unlike anyone else he could think of, she cared about what he did. Even though she'd questioned him and his motives in the beginning, she'd put her trust in him and it made his chest swell. He raised his arms wide. "Look at what you've achieved, look how hard you've worked to get such incredible results in such a short time. How could anyone not think that what you've done today is a great thing?"

"I guess, I didn't get it in the beginning," she said, "but

I've definitely seen how hard you work, and I feel like we're really starting to get results."

Results? She looked incredible, sounded incredible, and he couldn't hide how good that felt. Not for his own pride, but for the way she was beginning to feel about herself. Right in this second, seeing Kirin Hart blossom from the inside was gold. "I've given up trying to justify what I do to my family, but hearing it from you means more than you'll know."

Kirin stood staring at the man in front of her who was suddenly filled with so much passion and so much fire she thought he might catch alight.

If she'd been attracted to him when he was all sexy-cool and aloof, now she could hardly think straight. It was as if he'd been bottling himself since they'd met. And now she was seeing a tiny part of the real Blake. It was mesmerizing. And she wanted more.

She placed the tray on the counter. "I love that you're so passionate about what you do, now that I understand it. Not only does it make me feel as though I'm in really good hands, but it makes me realize how much this means to you on a deeper level. In fact..." She clasped her hands together. "I've been thinking about how much progress you and I have made and what we need to do to take my confidence to the next step."

"What does that mean?" he said with a grin.

She moistened her lips, her heart starting to race as her last conversation with Ellie and Gwin played again in her head. Every thought she'd had in the last forty-eight hours pointed to this second and she breathed slow, trying to make sure she said things right.

In the end, she decided to just show him.

She leaned in and placed a kiss on the dead center of his warm lips. But he didn't move. His breath, cool and male, fanned across her face and she left her mouth where it was, the sudden horror that she was doing the wrong thing cycling through her. Finally, she leaned back and rolled the taste of him between her lips. "I've been thinking about what happened between us the other night. I think I was wrong."

He stood still, arms at his sides, his scent of fresh forests and spring breeze lingering on her skin. "Tell me more."

If she got this wrong, he'd be out of here, and she couldn't possibly carry this on by herself. Risking everything, she reached up to place both hands on his shoulders. Standing on tiptoe, she leaned in. "Make love to me."

His Adam's apple moved in a swallow. The corners of his mouth twitched, and his eyebrows lifted. He burned to touch her as much as she burned for him. It was written all over his face. "What's changed?" he asked.

She looked into his eyes. "I've realized that what you've been saying right from the start makes so much sense."

His jaw moved, but he said nothing.

"I don't know how to act like the sexy woman you believe is part of the real me, because I haven't made love for so long. In the last few days with what happened with Trent and the way you've shown you have faith in my choices, I've begun to feel I can trust you. And you shared something very personal with me just now that confirms I'm in really good hands. I told you right from the beginning that if we were going to get through this together, I needed to trust you. Now I can, and it could make all the difference."

He didn't move, so she ran her hands down his arms, the swell of individual muscles bunched beneath his shirt, the warmth of his skin as her fingers drifted lower. "How can I achieve a sexual awakening on my own? I need a willing partner, and I think you'd be perfect."

"You're talking about something temporary, right?"

"Just for the next eight days." He was actually considering it. Her blood heated.

"And when it's over we part as friends, not with any regrets or skeletons that could be aired in public."

"As long as I can trust you not to tell anybody about this either now or when it's ended." Her pulse beat high in her throat. "I can trust you, can't I?"

His eyes flashed as he took a step forward and pulled her to him, his palms on the bare skin of her back sending beats of heat through her body. "You're sure you want this?"

She slid her hand down the smooth cotton of his shirt and tipped her chin up to look in his face. "Even more than pie."

"Then of course you can trust me." He pushed a piece of hair back from her shoulder. "I'd have as much to lose if we get this wrong."

She sucked in a breath. Anticipation and something else beat in her belly. Something she hadn't felt in a long time. She was going to be seduced by the most desirable man on the planet. Right now. Quite possibly on this kitchen floor. "I want you, Blake. Now. Here."

He tilted her chin back and brought his lips down on her mouth, and she sank into the fleshy warmth of his kiss. His tongue teased along her lips and she opened herself to him, reveling in the sweet taste.

While his mouth worked magic, his hands moved higher until his fingers tangled in her hair.

"I want to feel all of you," she breathed.

"Me too."

Mouth hitching in a grin, he grabbed the edges of his shirt and pulled it over his head. When his gloriously naked top half was revealed, Kirin's jaw fell slack as her eyes were riveted. If she'd thought he was the eighth wonder of the world with clothes on, then his broad, bare chest was the ninth, his powerful shoulders the tenth, and his washboard stomach leading to narrow hips took every place from eleven through twenty.

"Now you." He took a step closer and laid both hands low on her hips, his fingers sneaking under the tight fabric of her top until they found bare flesh.

She sucked in a breath as he started to peel the top up and over her head. And then, inch by agonizing inch, he revealed her body.

Blinded for a second as the fabric dragged over her face, she squeezed her eyes tight and flicked them open to see Blake's hungry eyes grazing her body, his face reflecting her own desire. He threw the top aside, then grinned, sexy and slow.

"What?" Kirin said. "What is it?"

"The bra, it's not what I expected."

She looked down at the plain white cotton bra and lifted her arm across her chest, but he held both hands by her sides. "You're teasing me."

A thumb swept her jawline. "Teasing? Never. You couldn't be more perfect." He stepped closer, and when his fingers played across the soft fabric covering her breasts, she gasped.

"I haven't seen the panties yet." His thumb trailed a line down her stomach 'til he reached the waistband of her skirt. "And I don't like to be kept waiting."

Ripples of anticipation raced across her midriff, then fanned lower as he eased the skirt down and over her hips. His eyes stayed locked on hers while he pushed the fabric lower, and she stepped out of the skirt.

"I guessed they'd be matching, though." He ran a hand swiftly across her white panties and then cupped her face. "You're beautiful." He leaned in and kissed the skin of her neck, lifting the curtain of hair, and his lips roamed free. Desperate to taste him again, she pulled him closer. Hot and hungry, his mouth crushed hers, and he pushed her back into the counter.

His hands played wild over the plains and valleys of her torso, and in turn she moved palms over his muscular back. He lifted her onto the countertop, the soft cotton of her panties slide across the granite. A knife went clattering to the floor and a bowl of salt upended and spilled across the counter.

She smiled into his lips before he guided his tongue into her mouth. He groaned as her thighs wound around him and he pulled her to him.

"Are you disappointed?" she whispered. "That it's not black lace."

"Surprised." He lowered his head to inspect her bra more closely. "Certainly not disappointed."

The cotton cup was thin enough that her arousal was obvious, the erect bud of a nipple peeping through.

"I could wear black lace if you wanted me to," she whispered.

"The white cotton's doing plenty for me right now," he said. "And it's all you."

"You'll tell me what to do, won't you?" Kirin whispered. "I've never known if what I was doing was right, and it's been a really long time, and I've only known my husband."

The thought of him teaching her, finding out what she loved, sent a heated shiver down her spine.

"Oh, I think we can cover a few things." He laid a kiss on her breast.

She closed her eyes as the sensation of Blake's mouth on the cotton covered nipple caused her to moan. While his lips worked, his fingers pushed the straps of her bra down until the cotton cup fell forward and her breast was revealed.

"What if someone saw us," she murmured as his mouth joined the fleshy rise of her breast.

"You'd like that?" His breath on her damp skin scrambled her thoughts. "I can carry you over to that window and lay you out on the seat for everyone to see."

The thought of having sex with Blake in a public place, of him doing things to her that only she could see and feel while other people were oblivious, caused the dampness at her center to become a slick.

"Well...." she began, but he put a finger over her lips and then replaced it with his mouth. "You talk too much," he said. "And think too much."

She kissed him back, deep and long and powerful, reveling in the closeness, in the feeling that she was with someone whose only focus was on her.

His stubble grazed her mouth, and she sucked at his lip as if it were the flesh of a tropical fruit. "We can stop if you'd like," he said, as his hand trailed down her chest, then on to her belly button, and finally to the soft cotton of her panties. "Just say the word and we can stop right there. Lesson one doesn't have to be all the way."

His hand ran along the top of the elastic. "Ummmmm." Paralyzed by the sensations flowing through her, she could say nothing more.

"What did you say?" His breath tickled her ear as his finger moved around the edge of her panties. He stroked the soft, delicate skin of her inner thigh, and she moaned into his neck. His hand slid around to the front, and he began to stroke the aching part of her.

"I, ahhh..." she groaned.

"I didn't hear you." His finger began a rhythmic circle.

Heat rushed to her center, and a feeling of being outside her body took hold. "I said you're good at this." She could hardly moan the words out, the pressure of his finger increasing, the fire spreading to her belly and the tops of her thighs.

"The best." Suddenly his finger slipped under the fabric of the panties and the bliss of his skin against the most delicate part of her was torture.

"Give me everything," she said, "I want all of you now."

"No protection," he said. "And I'm not going to leave you here while I go upstairs. Besides, the first time is all about you. Come closer." She gasped as he slid her forward.

"Are you okay?" He leaned closer and captured her lips in a kiss at the same time as he slipped a finger inside. Her cry was muffled in the warmth of his mouth, and all she could concentrate on was how her muscles welcomed his finger at each thrust.

The rhythmic scrape of his chest hairs against the bare skin of her breasts was sweet torture. And she moaned.

"Let yourself go," he whispered. He thrust faster with his fingers, and with each new movement she felt herself tighten. She closed her eyes and let the sensations he was creating in her body build to a crescendo.

He placed his thumb on her clit, and she felt as if she could rocket across the kitchen. As he pushed deeper, his thumb moved in firmer and firmer circles until she couldn't tell which part of him was touching her where.

"Oh, God, Blake." Her mouth dried and beating waves coursed through her.

"I've got you, baby, I've got you." His finger thrust, and the press of his hand on her back deeper as he held her.

He kissed her neck, and she could feel the urgency in his movements, knew that he could feel her release coming. When it did, she held on tight as wave after wave of pulsing warmth overtook her until she shuddered in his arms. She rested her cheek against Blake's chest and let the pleasure beat through her blood.

Her breathing slowed, and she drifted back, Blake lifted his head from her shoulder and his probing gaze held hers. "Are you okay?"

"Okay?" She smiled, remnants of heat still pulsing through her center. "You could say that. I didn't quite expect to go from 0 to 100 during lesson one." She reached over and retrieved her top from the knife block. "And I didn't expect it to be all about me."

He smiled. "Eight days and eight nights? I'm sure there'll be time in there to find some pleasure together."

She moved to put the top on, but he stilled his hand on her arm. "Don't," he said. "I want to look at you some more. I've never had a mostly naked woman sitting on my counter with only a string of pearls on." She squirmed. It was one thing to have Blake do what he'd just done, but to sit naked in his kitchen and talk felt all wrong.

"I don't feel that comfortable," she said, suddenly aware that her stomach was folded over on itself when she sat this way. Before she could move, he'd cupped a breast in his hand but kept his eyes on her face. He grazed his thumb across her nipple while he spoke. "I want you to feel safe around me, Kirin. Confident enough to tell me what you want and what you like. If you prefer to put your clothes back on after making love, that's fine. Just know that I'll be imagining these beautiful breasts, thinking about the next time I can touch them, and remembering the taste of them on my tongue."

"Oooh!" Another powerful surge of warmth raced through her and she took a steadying breath. "Okay," she said. "I'll keep that in mind."

Before he could start anything more, Kirin pulled the top over her head, then slid off the counter and reached for her skirt. "That's certainly a nice image to leave with."

"Stay the night," he said as she began to look for the shoes she'd kicked off. He was lounging against the opposite counter now, a hungry look in his eye, as if he already had lessons two through five planned out.

"Really, we don't need to carry this on today. It's Sunday tomorrow. We should collect ourselves. There's only one more week to get things done."

"Which is exactly why you need to stay here tonight. We don't have much time." His green eyes darkened. "And we have a lot of work to do. We could spend the day in bed tomorrow. And anyway, you owe me some pie." His mouth quirked.

She met his gaze and grinned. "For some reason, I just don't feel stressed anymore, and my hunger seems to have gone away completely. Shall we say same time, same place tomorrow for lesson number two? And if you play your cards right, I might even cook you dinner."

8

"My God, Kirin, do you know how stunning you look?" Lucy sat across the table in a bar the following afternoon and stared open-mouthed. "I thought I was choosing your wardrobe from here on in. Where'd you get that dress?"

Kirin smiled. "At a little store close to my house in Santa Monica." She had one eye on Lucy and one eye on her mother flirting with the barman. Candi had turned up just before she'd left to meet Lucy, so she'd invited her for a drink, too. They'd chosen a tiny place in Venice Beach, and it was still only late afternoon, so there were very few people around. There was only one other couple in the bar, and they were outside on the deck.

"I've looked in the window of that store a million times, but I've always been terrified to go in," she said. "Those sale assistants look like well-clothed gazelles, and I've always felt like such a fashion chump. After I'd gone through the new publicity shots with Alex this morning and they weren't as bad as I'd thought, I got the courage up. I love it too."

She brushed her hand over the silky fabric of the

tangerine halter neck dress. It whispered when she walked, and she loved the way it floated on her skin. For the first time she could remember, she was experimenting with showing off the tops of her arms, her waist, and a little cleavage. A pair of enormous gold hoops in her ears and a thin white belt to complement the look. She couldn't wait to show Blake. She'd arranged to meet him at his apartment later, and the thrill of anticipating lesson number two swam in her veins.

"And your hair's stunning, too!"

Coming from the always radiant Lucy, it was such a beautiful compliment that Kirin glowed. They'd kept in touch since the clothes fitting, and Lucy had texted a few times and suggested new designers and new looks that might suit her. It was lovely to be out having a drink together. It was her first time in public since the Larry Williams disaster, and she was determined to hold her head high.

"I might not stay around with you gals for too much longer." Candi had arrived back from the bar with a tray of colorful cocktails. "Miguel's invited me to a salsa party tonight, and I'm tempted. I'll need to go home and change. He's a few years younger than me, but what the hell. Which reminds me…" She put a glass in front of Kirin and perched on a stool. "I hope you've taken that gorgeous young Blake to bed, Kirin. Shouldn't let a set of abs like that go to waste."

"Mom!" Fire surged to Kirin's face, and she shot a look at Lucy from under her lashes. "Don't talk like that!"

"Nobody is listening, and don't worry about Lucy." Candi swiped a hand in the air. "She and I already talked about Blake while you were away in the bathroom, and we think you two would be darling together."

Kirin reached a trembling hand for a drink, then put the glass to her lips. "Can we at least keep our voices down?"

"Lucy explained about him not wanting to be with a celebrity," Candi whispered, "but I'm sure we could get him to change his mind. He'd make beautiful babies. I knew that about your father as soon as I saw him."

Kirin tried not to grit her teeth as she spoke quietly. "Mom, someone like Blake would never be interested in a relationship with a woman five years older when he could have his pick of women. Right, Lucy?"

Her new friend looked at her intently but said nothing.

"Honey, I'm not saying the guy would want to be with you *forever*—none of them ever do. I just hope you're using him to your best advantage while you have him, that's all."

Despite the cool slide of the cocktail, Kirin's throat dried to dust. "It's . . . it's not like that," she stammered. "He's working for me, helping me with my image."

"And what an amazing job he's doing." Lucy jumped to her defense. "It won't be long before you don't need Blake Matthews anymore. You've chosen this beautiful dress yourself, done your hair just right. Blake's skills can only go so far, and then it's up to you to run with it."

Kirin's body thrummed at the memory of the skills Blake had impressed her with last night. "We're on a deadline, anyway," she said, throwing a frown at her mother. "The contract is only for another week."

Candi sighed. "I just don't understand you girls today. There's a handsome man rolling in dollars, and all you can think about is your career."

"I hired him to help me get my career back on track, Mom, and that's all."

"Well, he's done a better job than I gave him credit for.

You've got a whole new sparkle in your eye the last couple days."

Kirin coughed on her drink. "That's because I'm learning how to do all this myself. If I had to rely on Blake all the time, then when the project's finished I'd be back to square one. He's given me the spark, and so has Lucy with all the help she's given me, but I need to take this and run with it myself."

"That's such a great way to look at it," Lucy said. "Style isn't about what someone else tells you, it's about being given more choices, more possibilities and looking at things in a whole new way."

A dark-haired man with a carry bag over his shoulder was making his way toward their table, and Kirin's stomach flipped. *Press.* She could spot them a mile away.

"Excuse me, ladies," he said with a wide-toothed smile. "I'm Guyon Prince from Entertainment Hotshots and I wondered if you'd mind if I took your photo. It's been a while since we've seen you on the town, Kirin, and I'm sure your fans would love to see this new look."

"I'm sorry, we're busy," Lucy said, voice tight. "Kirin's just having—"

She was about to agree with Lucy, but then put a steadying hand on her friend's arm and spoke so only Lucy could hear. "I think I should do this. Blake wanted me to be seen with other women, having fun. Would you mind being in it too? It would mean a lot to me."

Lucy grinned. "Of course."

"It's okay, Guyon," Kirin said as she perfected her best photo smile. "Take it whenever you're ready, but I'd like my friend and my mom in the shot."

"Of course."

The three of them squeezed closer together on their stools, Kirin in the middle, and Candi and Lucy on either side.

When the photographer had taken a few shots and written down the names of Lucy and Candi, he thanked them and left.

That had really been okay. No nastiness, innuendos, or sarcasm. It was baby steps, but she might just be on the path to change after all.

"I'm gonna love you and leave you girls now." Candi pushed her chair in. "Lucy, would you try to talk some sense into this girl of mine? She's going to find herself all rusted up if she doesn't start getting some practice in. Blake's right at your fingertips." Lucy turned away to talk to the waitress, and Candi leaned closer. "Whatever happens with Blake, or any man, I want you to know how good it is to see you happy in yourself again, sweetheart. I didn't realize how much of a cloud you've been living under until you started to come out from under it. Do you know how proud I am of you?"

Kirin nodded and smiled. Even though she didn't play the mother card often, when Candi said something like this, it was priceless. "Thanks, Mom. I do feel like things are starting to turn a corner."

"See you, honey." She kissed Kirin on the cheek and waved to Lucy.

"I should go too," Kirin said. "Where there's one photographer there will be more, and I think I've used up all my courage for one day. I'll give you a lift home."

"She's quite something, your mom," Lucy said when they were settled in Kirin's hatchback.

"I love her." Kirin put on her seat belt. "But she drives

me completely bananas. Since she moved to the city to be closer to me, she's gotten back into her painting, and she's doing really well. I just wish she'd be happy in her own skin and not think that having a man is the path to every kind of happiness."

"It's a bit of an easy trap to fall into, though." Lucy sighed and gave Kirin a rueful smile.

"Oh my God! Don't start talking like that. You're amazing, and you'll meet an amazing guy when the time's right."

"So will you."

Kirin turned. "No, a proper relationship's not going to happen for me again. Blake's taught me how to focus on myself and my solo brand. If I'm to create the sort of success I've had in the past, I have to be solo, in all senses of the word. Having a relationship could put everything I've worked for in jeopardy again."

Lucy bit her lip. "Then why would you sleep with Blake? I saw the way you reacted when your mom asked. It's none of my business, honey, and you know how dreamy I think Blake is, but do you really think you're doing the right thing?"

For a second, she considered denying Lucy's accusation, but she didn't want to lie to a woman who'd done so much for her and was becoming a friend.

"It's a fling, which is all I want from now on. And we're being super careful." She pushed the ignition. "What harm can it do?"

"Are you kidding me?" Despite them being in a car and the fact that there was no one else around, Lucy dropped her voice. "The whole reason for you having this makeover was because of what happened with that Trent creep. What if you guys get found out? It could be the very last straw for your career, and for Blake's. And apart from all that…" She hesitated, as if weighing up how much to say. "Blake's the center of his world, Kirin. His image and his business are everything to him. I don't know if he'd treat you that well."

Kirin tapped her hand on the steering wheel. "You see, that's where I think you're wrong, and so is everyone else I've spoken to about Blake. People think he's vain and self-absorbed, but I haven't found that at all since I've got to know him. He's been interested in me, interested in my life, he's met my mother."

Lucy nodded. "I hate to break it to you, but you *are* paying him. He's really your employee. Of course he's going to tell you what you want to hear. I'm not saying he's not being honest when he compliments you, but it's his job to get you feeling good about yourself. How much do you really know about him?"

She thought back to their conversations. "I know he's from a farm, in Oregon or Minnesota or somewhere. I know he's been a model since he was sixteen."

Lucy shook her head as another frown creased her brow. "I could've told you all that stuff by Googling him. Has he spoken to you about his relationships with other people, his friends, how much contact he has with his family?"

"Oh, come on, Lucy." She shifted in her seat. "Have you never had a fling with a guy just for fun?" She shook her head and laughed. "What am I saying? *I've* never done this sort of thing before, but it feels great, really great and I think you're over-analyzing it."

Lucy put her hand on Kirin's arm. "I just want you to look out for him, all right? Blake Matthews is all about Blake Matthews, and I'd hate for you to get hurt."

"I promise I'll be careful." Kirin released the brake. It was lovely of her friend to be so concerned. But she knew enough about Blake. Had spent so much time with him in the last week. And why shouldn't she have a bit of fun for once? They'd agreed on the terms of this relationship, knew exactly what it was for each other. It wasn't like anyone was going to get hurt, was it?

"Wow! Turn around."

Kirin stood in Blake's entranceway and twirled. Her conversation with Lucy had spurred her to keep this date with him. That, and the crazy need to show off in her dress.

As she spun back towards him, the spark in his eye sent pride rolling through her body. "You approve? You like it?"

"I do approve. Wait there a second." He moved into the lounge room and came back with the Polaroid. "This is for the keeper folder."

She threw an arm high in the air, struck a pose and laughed. He took a picture, she turned to her other side, and he took another before putting the camera on the hall stand as it spat out the photos.

Inky jeans clung to muscular thighs, and a clearly defined chest was outlined by a plain white t-shirt. Tingling warmth began in her fingers as she anticipated touching him above and underneath the shirt.

"You couldn't have chosen a better style," he said, still standing at arms-length. "I especially like the way it..." He reached out a finger and ran it, oh so slowly, from her chin, down her neck, stopping at the point of the V.... "dips here."

Heat rippled from where the tip of his finger touched her, out towards her nipples budding beneath the silky fabric. His finger stroked up and down, the heat rolling from her breasts to her belly, and becoming a dull throb between her legs. His eyes darkened. "I've never seen you wear something so revealing. But I want to see less of the dress and more of you."

Closer. All she wanted was to be closer to him, but her legs were lead, her body transfixed by the steady rhythm of his finger.

"It's a beautiful dress," he said, voice sexy-low. "Lift your hair for me." Although the shadows in his eyes gave some hint to what he had planned for her, his face was impassive, as if he knew that taking his time would drive her wild.

She put her hands beneath her hair and lifted it off her shoulders, the fabric of the dress grazing her aching nipples as it rode higher.

"Perfect." He grinned. "If only we had an alligator clip to hold it there."

She bit her lip, his joke easing the sprint of her heart for a second, but when he took a step closer, it resumed double time. "Lesson one seems to have had a significant effect on you. I can't imagine what you're going to pull out of the bag after lesson two. Turn around."

She did as she was told and in the next minute his fingers were working the bow at her neck until the fabric loosened and fell away at the front. She was standing in Blake Matthews's apartment, naked from the waist up, and all she could concentrate on was the need to have his hands running over her body.

When he hugged her from behind and placed both hands on her stomach, she shivered in anticipation. Slowly, he slid his touch up until both hands cupped her breasts. "Here was me looking forward to that sexy white bra, and you go and surprise me by not wearing one."

She couldn't stop the moan that slid from her mouth as

his hands molded her breasts and his thumbs tweaked her needy nipples.

He leaned in and kissed her hair, and when she tipped her head back to his broad shoulder, she breathed the freshly showered scent of him deep. He slid his hands to her waist again, and she shivered when he eased the zipper down. Gripping each side of the dress, he peeled the silky fabric the length of her body until it pooled at her feet.

He reached around her again, but this time slipped a hand in hers and turned her to face him. He stepped forward and the slow, deliberate movements were replaced by a frenzy of touch as his hands tangled in her hair, and she twined her arms around his neck. When he claimed her mouth, the kiss was harder, hungrier than before, and the thought that he wanted her as much as she wanted him powered through her like a drug.

Their chests pressed together, and she felt his heart, beating as deep and strong as hers.

Still kissing him, she burrowed her hands under his t-shirt and sighed as her palms met the hard planes of his stomach. Greedily, she pushed the fabric up, and he helped tug it over his head.

"The window seat," she gasped. "Take me on the window seat."

"No way," he growled. "Public sex is lesson three, and I'd hate for you to miss out on all the treats of lesson two. This one happens in my bed."

He bent down, scooped her effortlessly into his arms, and she leaned her forehead against his. "You're going to put me out of a job if you're not careful," he murmured in her ear as he mounted the stairs. "That dress was a knockout."

"Must be the skills of my very fine teacher." She smiled,

and he captured her mouth in a kiss as they reached his bedroom.

He strode to the bed, threw back the covers, and laid her out. He slipped her shoes off then stepped back, unbuckled his jeans and kicked them to the floor, his white boxers following seconds later.

Suddenly she found a brand new candidate for the eighth wonder of the world. His erection stood proud and rigid at his center, and she couldn't wait to have it pressed against her. She moved to sit up, but he gently pushed her back and then eased his body alongside her.

She pushed her panties down and kicked them off before tangling her legs with his. Holding her face, he kissed her deep. His tongue plundered her mouth, and she hungered for every piece of him. The touch of his rigid length against her thigh emboldened her to snake a hand down and take the warm, solid shaft in her grip.

"Ah, baby," he moaned, and she stroked him harder as he lay a trail of kisses down her neck.

He rolled her underneath him, then placed his hands either side of her head. Above her, he blinked slowly as he opened her thighs with his knee, and she gasped at the hungry look in his eye. Kissing a line from her neck, he paused to lay a reverent kiss on each nipple, then down, down to the very core of her.

His breath was hot against her thigh, and she sucked in a breath of anticipation. When his lips met her swollen folds, she floated off the bed. Never before had someone touched her so intimately, and with such open desire. She couldn't help the private smile on her lips as Blake's tongue took her on a journey she'd only dreamed about.

His lips worked her bud while his tongue laved her opening, and she clutched at the sheets in ecstasy. Slowly a wave built, and she fought it, desperate to wait until she could look in Blake's eyes, let him see what he could do to her. Paralyzed on her back, she murmured, "My turn."

"Still mine." He leaned over to the bedside table, pulled out a foil packet and in seconds had sheathed himself. In an exquisite kissing journey, he moved up her body, leaving her damp and open and desperate. As he reached her mouth and trapped her lips in a kiss, he eased himself inside her.

Air squeezed from her lungs as Blake's length filled every empty part of her. He buried himself deep, and she arched her back to get even closer.

Her skin was on fire—a fire which spread up her thighs and deep inside, joining with the thick, thrusting end of Blake.

Sliding an arm under her shoulders, he pulled her to him and thrust faster. In turn, Kirin gripped him and pulled each muscle tight as the wave of pleasure built.

Blake's eyes grew darker, the sheen on his skin glowed, and he called her name in a rush of breath before his rhythm slowed and he rested his cheek against hers.

Her eyes fluttered closed, great, rolling waves of pleasure taking her under, and she left her body far behind.

Long moments of silence, except for the gradual easing of their breathing, hung in the air until Blake spooned her and hugged her tight.

It could have been minutes or hours later when Kirin uncurled herself from his side and turned to him. "I don't suppose a girl gets to repeat a lesson, does she? I think there were a few parts I may need to practice."

"Of course that's possible," Blake said, "but while she's practicing lesson two, a girl would be missing out on all that lesson three has to offer."

"The public sex?" she whispered as she pulled a sheet

over their bottom halves and snuggled into him again. "She might be content with lesson two for the rest of her life then."

"A girl would need some lead up to lesson three." He slid a hand between her legs. "Perhaps a little fondling under a table, or a friendly kiss that went on a little too long."

She chuckled, then looked into his face, wanting to keep things light but needing more of a connection, too. "Thank you for this. I really think it's hitting the spot, so to speak."

He lifted an eyebrow. "You're very welcome."

"I had cocktails with Mom and Lucy tonight and Mom suggested that I should have bedded you by now."

"She's quite the character, your mom."

Kirin circled a finger on his chest. "What's your mom like?"

He frowned. "You don't want to talk about my family. Especially not after what we just did."

"I do. You told me where you come from and a little about your business background, but nothing else. I'd like to know a little more about you."

"What for?"

Her skin chilled at his tone. "Because we've . . . at least I hope we have . . . become friends, and friends tend to know a bit about each other."

"Don't take this the wrong way, but I'm not interested in talking about myself. You and I have a great business relationship, and we're having a nice time on the side, but that's as far as it goes. I'm not my family or my past. I'm my business, and *you're* my business. I thought we'd had this conversation before."

Kirin clutched the sheet in her hand and pulled it a little higher. He was charismatic, devastatingly good-looking, an incredible lover, and as guarded as a bank vault.

Warning bells went off to not ask anything else, but it wasn't in her nature to stay quiet. "What about friends then?" She wanted to push him on this, peel back a little of that perfect exterior to see what was underneath. "Do you hang out with Lucy and Colin, have a beer with Alex sometimes?"

He pushed himself up against the headboard and he turned to face her again. "What's all this about?"

"You've met my dog, my mom, you know my sexual history and how many salt shakers I own, and yet I realize now that I don't really have a handle on who you are at all." She dragged herself up too, but kept the sheet tucked under her arms. "I've never heard you talk about friends. You don't seem to have any hobbies—apart from the ones that make you look good—and it seems as though you hardly live here. "

He reached out a finger and stroked her cheek as his tone softened. "You have all the bits of me you need, Kirin. Those are the ones you should be concerned about. Come here and stop worrying. We have a whole week left, and I intend for it to be spent focusing on you, not me."

As he nuzzled her neck and his hands searched for her under the sheet, she let her eyes drift closed. Why did she feel she needed to know more about him? Was it to disprove other people's impressions and confirm he wasn't the superficial man only concerned with looks as they'd have her believe? Because if she did believe what they said, it might make it easier to ignore the deeper feelings she had for him that were growing day by day.

Blake buried his head further into the pillow and stretched into the mattress, hoping to connect with the warm, lush contours of Kirin's body as he'd done all night. Finding the spot next to him empty, he drifted his hands across the sheet and his fingers curled around a small piece of cardboard. In seconds, he was fully awake.

Dull sunlight peeked through the curtains, giving just enough light to see what he was holding. An instant camera print, and by the stage of development it was at, he guessed it hadn't been taken long ago.

It was him. Buck naked and tangled in the sheets. Sprawled on his back with his mouth slightly open, he looked relaxed, off guard. The thought of Kirin standing naked and watching him sleep while she took the photo was almost as hot as last night.

His skin was tender from where she'd raked her nails down his back, his lips roughened from kissing her all night long, and other parts of him still hummed where she'd sheathed him. For a woman who hadn't made love in a long time, she sure knew how to get back on that horse with style.

He swung his legs over the side of the bed and scrubbed hands through his hair. If anyone had told him a week ago that Kirin Hart would be sharing his bed on his next available weekend, he'd have laughed them out of the room. But he didn't regret it for a second. Lying awake into the early hours, talking and holding her close had felt damn good, and he couldn't wait for it to happen again. But their time was running out fast.

He stared at a spot on the wall. When their time together was over, Kirin would be too busy focusing on the new success of herself as an independent businesswoman to have room in her life for any sort of relationship, in fact being on her own for the near future would keep the focus firmly on her as it should be. And he'd be on the other side of the country, managing the enormous corporation she'd helped him acquire. When this deal was over, there would be no more long nights of holding her close, no more evenings cooking in her warm kitchen. Suddenly, only seven days more together seemed far too few.

He dragged on a pair of boxers and padded down the stairs. When he saw her working behind his kitchen counter, he stopped dead. Damn, it always put him off balance when he watched her cook.

Stepping back into the shadows, he reveled in the sight of her. She wore one of his business shirts, sleeves rolled to the elbow and short enough that the curve of one butt cheek was visible. A smile tugged at his mouth. She'd caught her hair back in an alligator clip that she'd obviously had in her bag, and odd sections of hair brushed past her face.

And she was humming. A low, slow tune that made him want to sit here and listen all day long.

"Seen enough?" She looked up with a cheeky smile. He'd been caught. "I'm making frittata if you'd like some. Have you ever cooked in here? Most of your utensils were still in their plastic wrappers."

He took the last few stairs. "If God had wanted me to cook, he wouldn't have invented burger joints. It's far too early to eat, but what's in the frittata?" He moved closer and the aroma of browned butter and Kirin filled his senses.

"I'd usually take leftovers from the refrigerator and cook them with some really fresh eggs and tasty cheese. You didn't have any leftovers, so I did some sweet potato and spinach. You'll like it."

He stood behind her and reached around to her front.

The feel of her breasts, lush and warm under the cotton of his shirt, her body pressed close, was all he needed for breakfast. "Blake, I'm cooking!" She giggled, and he couldn't stop himself from nudging her butt.

"And I'm hungry," he whispered close to her ear, "but not for your cooking."

He nuzzled her neck, and she laid her cheek back on his. "I have a little surprise for you," he said, "and it's not what you're feeling against you right now. I managed a pretty big coup yesterday that I was going to tell you about last night, but I kind of got distracted. I'll tell you when we sit down."

Despite the fact he hardly ever ate breakfast, he couldn't stop his mouth watering from the sight and smell of what Kirin was dishing up. When she'd brought the plates to the table, they sat down and she reached for the coffee. "So, I can't bear the excitement. What is it?"

He picked up a fork. "Remember that list you gave me right at the beginning of our contract when I asked what you wanted to happen most?"

She looked up, her wild-honey eyes round and questioning. "Yes."

He dug into the eggy mixture. "What was top of your list?" He put the fork in his mouth and almost groaned at the explosion of rich, cheesy goodness.

"I don't know." She shrugged. "My debts coming down, having the chance to cook a big event again."

"Stop right there."

She put her hand on his arm, her eyes glistening and the warm memory of her touching him everywhere last night, firing him on. "There's a charity dinner for eight hundred people at the Venice Ballroom Friday night. Jean-Pierre Marcand was supposed to lead the team of chefs but he's come down with an infection from a cut to his hand. It's yours if you want it, but I need to confirm today."

Her cheeks paled as her dusky lips opened slowly. "The Venice Ballroom? For 800? In place of Jean-Pierre Marcand, are you serious? Oh, God, Blake, how can I ever thank you!"

In the next second, she'd thrown herself into his lap and was kissing him. He slid a hand across her shoulders, but she pulled back, eyes crinkling with laughter. "A week, no— five days to get this organized? This is *insane*, but my absolute dream come true!"

Her cheeks glowed, her eyes sparkled, and Blake's chest swelled at the realization he'd caused the reaction. The tops of her legs brushed his, and he breathed the scent of her mixed with him in his shirt.

She kissed his cheek again and slid off his knee to pace the floor. "There's so much to organize! I'll need to review the staff, go to the venue, speak to Jean-Pierre."

"It'll be fine," he said, missing the feel of her against his body. "Come eat your eggs. You're going to be busy. There are a couple other things I'm hoping will come through today, but this will be our priority for now. Jean-Pierre will walk you through everything. People who paid for the dinner were expecting him so the organizers will be relieved to have someone with an equal profile."

She suddenly stopped pacing and pressed her steepled fingers to her lips. "Will they be disappointed? After all my bad publicity, the fact I haven't had a profile in so long, will the guests feel ripped off?" Doubt clouded her eyes.

"It's a perfect opportunity for your launch back onto the cooking stage. A captive audience of food lovers who also have big hearts and big wallets. We'll build your profile with the new publicity shots this week to the extent that people will be dying to see you by the time Friday rolls around. You'll stun them."

She threw him a smile—the most heartfelt, open smile he'd ever received from anyone, and it rocketed straight to his chest. And then the feeling was gone, replaced by a widening hole. In a little over a week, Kirin Hart would have won back her public, signed off with Dent and Douglas, and become exactly what she wanted to be—a woman who didn't need someone like him. And that wasn't what he wanted anymore.

9

The next afternoon, Kirin stepped from Blake's elevator into his penthouse. Registering the broad shoulders turned away from her at the kitchen counter, excited words burst from her.

"You'll never guess who called. I couldn't believe it when I heard her voice. I was so busy with Jean-Pierre that I didn't imagine my day would get any better, but it did as soon as she spoke." She turned to hang her cotton jacket on a coat hook and heard him move in the kitchen. "Only the hottest daytime talk show host in California. And she wants me as a live guest Monday!" Her voice began to run away as she tried to get the words out. "I know you engineered all this, but it still felt like the best surprise. I've met Felicity Farrell before and I'm sure . . . Blake?" He hadn't answered. "Hey, what's wrong?" She moved to the doorway.

The man at the counter faced her, and she gasped. He stood like Blake, powerful and confident, had the same dimple at the corner of his mouth, the same chestnut hair, but his face was damaged. It was as if someone had dragged a huge paintbrush down his cheek and left a long, withering scar.

Kirin swallowed, her brain too scrambled to form words, mouth too dry.

He held out a hand and stepped forward. "I'm Bryn, Blake's brother."

Unbidden, her eyes stayed fixed on the scarring of his right cheek as she shook his hand. Had he been in an accident? Born like that? It could've been a burn by the way the skin was shiny in some parts and ridged and corded at others. And why had she not known Blake had a brother? A twin? So exactly like him in every other detail.

Her insides caved. She'd spent the last week with Blake. He'd made love to her on his countertop, in his bed, knew every detail about her life. He'd become so important to her, and yet she knew nothing about him at all.

"I'm sorry, I shouldn't have walked in like that." She motioned back to the door. "Blake gave me a key, and I wasn't expecting..."

"I've only just arrived from the airport myself." He moved back to the counter and the coffee machine. "The concierge checked if it was okay to let me up. My brother's too busy to meet me until later, apparently. We can wait for him together."

Kirin swallowed. "I didn't realize Blake had a twin . . . I mean he didn't speak about you."

"I'm not surprised." He picked up a coffee cup. "Blake and I might've looked identical once, but that's where our similarities end." He pointed to his face. "As you can imagine, I don't fit into his lifestyle so we don't spend a whole lot of time together."

"That's a shame." Should she go? The undertow of animosity indicated Bryn wasn't here on a social call.

"Please tell Blake I dropped by with some news. I'll call him later."

"You don't have to go," he said. "Blake shouldn't be too long. Why don't I make some coffee? I flew here after a twelve-hour shift, and I need some java to keep me awake."

Intrigued to have an opportunity to find out the details about Blake and his family that he wouldn't tell her himself, she decided to ask a little more. "Sure, coffee would be lovely, thanks." She pulled up a stool. "What do you do?"

"I'm a surgeon. From Long Island." He smiled. "And no, not a plastic surgeon. I specialize in microsurgery of the hands."

"Oh, wow." It felt a little strange questioning Bryn, but right in this moment she had an insatiable need to find out more about his brother, the man who'd learned about her deepest fears, had explored every inch of her body. She couldn't pass the opportunity up. "That must be incredibly rewarding work."

"It is. It's fantastic to be able to help people when they've been through such trauma." He spooned coffee into the espresso machine.

"I guess it's tough to see much of Blake when you're so busy and you guys live so far apart."

He shrugged. "We only live an hour from each other but I haven't seen him in four years."

She frowned. "Oh, I'm sorry, I thought you said you lived in Long Island."

"I do. Not far from Blake in Manhattan."

A chill swept her veins. A twin brother she'd had no idea about, and Blake didn't actually *live* here? She thought about what he'd promised her two nights ago. That she could trust him in everything he did and said. Did that include everything he didn't do and didn't say as well? About his family? Where he really lived? Obviously not.

She spoke quickly to hide her surprise and hurt. "So, what's he doing in San Francisco?"

"Trying to sort some major fashion crisis, I expect. Are you his girlfriend?"

Heat touched her cheeks. "Oh. No, I'm the crisis that needs sorting." She tried to lighten the mood. "Blake's helping me get my mojo back."

Bryn shoved a hand in his pocket. "Hey, I'm sorry, that was rude of me." He flicked the switch on the machine and a low rumble began, followed by the smell of freshly brewed coffee. "Tell me about your work with Blake. I've never really understood what he does."

He looked at her intently, and she sensed sadness in his eyes, as if he really didn't know his twin at all, and wanted to find out about Blake as much as she did.

"I've had a bit of a PR crisis with my business and Blake's turned around my image in less than ten days. I'm very grateful to him. He's got a reputation for being one of the best image consultants in the industry so I'm very lucky."

"That's great. You must be pleased."

At war with herself over whether to end the conversation here out of a sense of loyalty, or dig deeper, she let curiosity win over.

"Are you here for long?"

He flicked another switch and frothy milk poured into the two cups. "Just long enough to get something from my brother. I need to get back to work, so I'm hoping he won't keep me waiting long. I'd like him to make a trip back to our home state with me."

He passed her the cup, and she wrapped her hands around it. "Oregon, isn't it?"

"That's right. Mom and Dad are on a farm there, but they're getting too old to cope. I'd like for us to get them somewhere smaller and more manageable."

Half an hour later, Kirin put her cup back on the counter. Blake hadn't arrived and she and Bryn had reached the end of their polite discussions about cooking and what it was like moving to a big city from a small town. She'd gained no more insight into Blake's early life, or why he hadn't seen his brother for four years.

Bryn seemed as closed and secretive as his brother, and it only made her want to know more about the rift that was so obvious between them.

"I'm sorry you didn't get to see Blake," Bryn said.

"I'll be catching up with him later on, so it's not a problem. It was really nice to meet you, Bryn. I hope we get another chance to catch up before you leave."

"I'd like that," he said as he walked her to the door. "But I'm hoping I won't need to be here after today, so maybe another time. Good luck with all your new changes. I'm glad everything's working out for you."

They said goodbye and Kirin stood with the closed door at her back. She might only have a few days more left with him, but Kirin had a burning desire to find out all there was to know about Blake Matthews, the man who she'd given every part of herself to in the past ten days. He'd helped tear down the walls she'd had up for so long, and she wanted that for him, too. Whether he liked it or not, that's exactly what she was going to do.

"Bye, Kirin, keep practicing!"

Kirin waved goodbye to Lucy and her sister Pippa, who'd

given her another make-up lesson, and closed her front door. She leaned her head against the wooden frame and summoned the courage to walk into her living room and confront Blake about what she'd found out from Bryn yesterday.

Blake had called and suggested she come by last night, but something had made her say no—a gnawing feeling that she didn't really want to know the truth about him. That if she kept this relationship they had as casual as he wanted it to be, then none of this mattered.

But it mattered to her. She wanted to know that the man she'd opened herself up to in so many ways wasn't a liar or a heartless brother. She'd seen something in Blake when she'd first met him, a wariness, as if he was guarding a private part of himself, but he'd let her see inside him in the last few days, and she hungered for more. Despite alarms going off in her head, she had to have it out with him.

"Pippa and Lucy are great together, aren't they?" she said, walking back into her living room and sitting on the edge of the couch. She was bulldozing her way to the subject, but too bad. "It must be nice to have a sibling you feel that close to. Flynn and I are close but haven't lived near each other in years, so it's extra special when we get together. Do you have close siblings?"

"Not so you'd notice."

Blake sat down beside her on the couch, and Dudley wandered over to lie on the floor at their feet. She reached down and scratched behind his ears.

"Have I told you how much that top suits you?" He curled a finger under one of her shoestring straps. "I think it would suit being thrown in a pile on the floor, too."

She moved her shoulder a little, wanting him to concentrate on what she was saying. "Is that a yes or a no?"

He shrugged. "I have three brothers. None of us are close."

"They don't live near you?"

"One lives close." He tilted his head. "In the next state, anyway."

"In Nevada, back home in Oregon?"

His brows moved lower, and he shot her a dark look. "You've met my brother, haven't you?"

She twisted so she could see him better, and now her knee touched his thigh. "I came by your apartment yesterday. He seemed a little uptight."

He sat back on the couch. "Bryn doesn't like anyone much." He played with the stitching on the back of a cushion. "You know what I could kill for right now is some of that pasta with the green stuff on top."

He thought she didn't notice when he tried to divert attention from himself? He was wrong. "What happened to his face? Was he burned?"

He sighed. "Scott, my eldest brother was supposed to be watching us when we were four but he was making out with his girlfriend instead. Bryn fell against a bar heater and received third-degree burns. It completely changed our family. Mom spent weeks away in the city with him while he was recovering, and then there were lots of operations to try and fix the damage to his face."

"It must be difficult for him, having the scars so obvious."

He nodded. "Of course it is. He's happier now that I'm not around so he doesn't need to be reminded about the way he could've looked."

"That must be so hard for him." *And you.*

"Hard for everyone. Why else do you think I was so desperate to get off the farm and away from them all? Not only was I a reminder to him about what he'd lost, but my parents as well. Mentioning anything about the way you looked in our family became so taboo, I couldn't even tell my parents why I was leaving home. The fact I made my money and my name from perceived beauty was an insult to them when they found out. Still is."

Kirin reached out a hand and laid it on his rigid arm, wanting to connect with him now that he was opening up. He must have felt so alone as a little boy. "So why's he here if you guys don't get along?"

"He wants me to go back home to try to persuade Mom and Dad to go into a retirement home. And I will as soon as I'm finished with this project. I told him as much on the phone, and texts, but he seems to think talking face to face will change my mind about going sooner. It didn't. He's going back tomorrow."

Kirin's heart ached for Blake and what the family had been through. It was no wonder he was so defensive about his looks and the business he'd created. The reasons for him being so closed, so distrustful of his inner-self, were easy to see now. "Bryn also told me you live in New York, not San Francisco. Why would you keep something like that from me?" Hurt pulsed like tiny daggers in her veins.

"I don't work for Dent and Douglas." He shifted in his seat. "I want to buy their business, but they wouldn't sell while their reputation was suffering under you. I should've told you from the beginning, but you took some convincing, and I thought it was an unnecessary complication. That you'd think my priority was a quick solution rather than the right solution if I told you the truth."

Her chest hollowed. "So your mission was to turn me around and then they'd sell?"

"Yes." His eyes were downcast.

"And you led me to believe it was because you were so concerned about the state of my career." She frowned as everything started to become clear. "And it wasn't about me at all. It was about you and your career."

He leaned closer, but she sat straighter, hugging herself, heart cracking. "And if you couldn't turn me around? If you didn't manage to soften my hard edges, drag me kicking and screaming into the twenty-first century, then what?" Her voice shook. "You'd lose the only thing that matters to you—building your empire?" How could she have been so naïve to think she was his sole focus? She was nothing more than a ticket to his success. She'd been in that position before, but this time it felt a whole lot worse.

He ran his hand up and down her arm, and little shivers raced through her body. "It's not going to happen. We have some great publicity shots, the charity dinner, the Felicity Farrell interview. You're doing incredibly well. I couldn't be more proud of you."

Despite the warmth in his eyes and his flattering talk, her throat closed. "I feel as though I've been used."

He continued the slow back and forth slide up her arm, and he let out a chuckle. "Used? How? You signed a contract, knew the time constraints. How have I used you?"

"You haven't told me the truth. Either about what this project means to you, or who you really are." Her jaw tightened, her pulse to harden, and a slow anger bubbled up from the deepest part of her. "I trusted you, Blake. I put my whole self—the way I look, the way I act, how I make love—I put all those things into your hands. But before I did that I asked if I could trust you and you looked me in the eye and told me yes. Why would you lie to me?" She swatted angry tears.

His hand stilled on her arm. "Kirin, I'm sorry," he said. "I should've told you earlier about D and D, and me only visiting here, but it changes nothing. In fact, I think it's helped."

"How on earth has it helped?" She moved her arm from under his, the sudden loss of connection she'd felt building over the last few days sitting raw and wounded in her chest.

"I didn't tell you about what I had to do to buy D and D because it would've been too much pressure on you. You had enough to cope with. What you suffered with Trent Bray, all the media interest, the Larry Williams show, and the sex tape. All along you've thought you were doing all this for yourself, not for me, and look what you've achieved. By focusing on you, the media interest has died down, you're getting out and about again, and anyone who sees you knows your confidence has been boosted out of sight."

She frowned, but waited for him to explain more.

"This whole project has been about us focusing on you, not me. That's why I didn't tell you about my professional goals, or about my life outside work. This has, and always will be, all about you."

He leaned forward and pressed his lips to hers, and the familiar fizz through her blood took hold. What he said was true. This had never been about him, or even the two of them. It was only about her and what he could do with her. He'd never promised her anything different, but it didn't stop the empty feeling that was growing deep inside.

Maybe this would just have to be part of her awakening as well. Learning she could share her body with someone, be close without investing anything more. It ran against everything she'd always believed in, but it was all Blake had to offer.

Could she take the risk of not falling for him? Or would

she ever be satisfied that he truly didn't have anything to give her, and this was all it would be?

He pulled back and held her face in his hands. "When I first met you, I couldn't have imagined how far you'd come, but I think it's a credit to both of us that we're at the stage where we're almost ready to launch you back into the world."

She swallowed and stitched on a smile. There were only five days left in the contract. Five days for her to fulfill her end of the bargain, and then their time together would be over. She cleared her throat "So what's left for you to do?"

Blake's face lit up. "I'll be presenting to D and D next Monday afternoon, directly after the Felicity Farrell interview, and if that's gone well and all the other indicators are good then I'll get to buy my company."

"Which means you'll be heading back to New York."

"Yes, but it also means five whole nights of us being together before that. And I don't want to waste a single one of them."

He leaned in to kiss her again, and when she opened herself up to him, he laid her back on the couch. He was right. There were only five days and nights left until Blake got what he wanted. She was a means to his business end, and the fact he'd kept that from her burned. But things were different now. She'd seen a tiny part of the real Blake, and she wanted so much more.

"So, what are you going to do about Bryn?" Kirin said, reaching for the coffee Blake had just brought her. He'd been reluctant to leave the bed after they'd made love this morning, but there was a lot to do today. Seeing her now with her halo of hair and her freshly flushed skin, he wanted to take the cup from her hands and lay her body out again.

"Do? About what?" He settled himself beside her.

"He leaves for Salem tonight, doesn't he? Don't you think you two should get something sorted?"

He stretched his legs out in front and flexed his feet. "He shouldn't have turned up here. I've already told him I'll help sort things when I have enough time to give it the attention it deserves."

"Which will be when?" Her gaze held steady on his face. He thought they'd put his family and his past to rest last night. "It's complicated. I'll do it when it's time."

She dropped her voice to the soothing tone she used with Dudley, and his spine stiffened. "I've been the recipient of your *own time*, Blake, and it can be frustrating. And actually quite rude."

He shrugged. "I get busy."

Kirin put her dusky lips to the rim of the cup and sipped. "What you do is you make people wait until you're ready, and it can give the impression you don't care. Deep down, I know you do."

Guilty as charged. And he'd done it to remind her who was in charge, but he hadn't done it in a long time. He shifted uncomfortably. It seemed arrogant and controlling now, and that's not the way he wanted to be anymore. The truth was, these days he couldn't wait to be wherever Kirin was.

"You're wrong, I don't care." He shrugged. "And I thought we had an agreement not to get into each other's lives outside work anymore."

She was quiet for a second. "You know I love talking about food and clothes and what's next on the agenda, but since you've helped me out so much, I want to help you too."

She put her coffee on the nightstand and turned toward him. As she did, the sheet slipped lower and one sweet breast was exposed. That she didn't try to cover up filled him with pride, because she was open and exposed around him and it made him want to do everything he could for her, for as long as he could.

"Feeling that your family can't celebrate your success, that they don't see what you do as worthy must have had a profound impact on you. But cutting all ties and not having them as part of your life must have a profound effect too."

His hand tightened around the coffee cup. "It is what it is. I know no different."

"I do," she said quietly. "I know there's a whole lot hiding inside here." She ran two fingers across his heart, and he stiffened. "Stuff you're too scared to let out, and I think if you did you'd be—"

He swung his legs over the side of the bed and stood. "I don't have time for this."

"You don't seem to have a lot of time for anything that involves you feeling too much. Or for people who challenge you." She stayed still, her sparkling eyes trained on his face. "And because I *do* feel, and you've helped me feel and experience more than I ever thought possible, I'm going to give you a few home truths."

Despite an overpowering urge to get out of here, away from Kirin's accusations and confident statements, his feet were rooted to the floor.

"You've taught me an unbelievable amount in the last ten days, Blake, not least of all that for most of my life I've been presenting an outer self that had little connection to my inner one. With your help, your attention, and sometimes your patience, I've worked on that and you've helped me redefine who I really am. Not a bad feat for a little over a week."

He shrugged lazily. "All part of the service."

He may as well have said nothing, because she kept right on talking. "Which brings me to your inner self."

He scoffed out a laugh, but she continued.

"I think you've spent so much of your life exposed, being picked over, complimented, bought, and sold, that you've guarded your inner self with a fierce power. And in the process of protecting yourself so much, you've alienated those around you. And you've missed out on having meaningful relationships."

He wanted to scoff again. Wanted to flick off her psychoanalysis with a laugh and a cutting comment, but he couldn't. The way she looked at him, with her open face and her caring smile, was enough to undo him. "Maybe I have done that to avoid any more crap from my family, but there's no way to undo what's been done. I still have my image business, and Bryn and my parents still hate me for it. Nothing's going to change, and no one cares about this but you."

She lay there, all lush and warm, but it wasn't her body that held him frozen. It was the openness in her eyes, as if she was inviting him into her soul. And he didn't know which way to run.

"I'm sure they don't hate you, but why not rise above the past? Why not give Bryn a date that you'll go home? You could leave Tuesday. Our time will be up then, and you can spend a couple days helping Bryn with your parents."

"Maybe." He thought ahead to Monday, the day his time with Kirin would be finished. She had the Felicity Farrell interview to do in the morning. He was certain she'd fly through. And then she'd be on her own, without the need for anymore advice.

Without the need for him.

She was blossoming into exactly what he'd wanted for her: a confident, sexy woman who had the world at her feet. "I don't know what good it'll do."

"It might make you feel as though you're putting the past behind you. What your family does with that is up to them but it's kind of like what we're doing with the Trent Bray thing now. The sex tape scandal's died a quiet death because we wouldn't stoop to his level. We've taken the higher ground, gotten on with things our *own* way. Determining *our* own future."

She was saying *our,* but she meant they were doing everything for her future. She was now on her own. Just as they'd agreed.

"Does it feel good to be out there on your own?" he asked.

"It didn't in the beginning. At first I wanted to make Trent pay, fight using the same old weapons, but you taught me differently, Blake. You showed me to make my own rules and I have. And it feels so good. We haven't heard about that wretched tape because we rose above it."

"You think my family will welcome me back with open arms?"

"Maybe not." She lifted her brows. "I don't always see eye-to-eye with my mom. In fact, she drives me completely crazy most of the time. But I couldn't imagine not having her in my life, not having a link to who I was. That's what really determines success, I think, being able to see where you've come from to know where you want to go. I think it's important for everyone, but especially for you."

Sun from the window threw light in her hair as she

spoke, and the glow reflecting off her warmed him to his core. He'd do just about anything Kirin Hart told him right now, especially if it meant keeping her in his bed a little longer.

"What I need is someone like you to come along and feed me my lines," he said, as he lay back down on his side, facing her. "And then we could go find something fun to do when I realized I'd made a terrible mistake in going back." He found her leg beneath the sheet and began to stroke it.

"Oh, no," she said with a teasing smile. "Other people's families are a whole different ball game. Ask me to cook for you and I'll have no hesitation, but other people's families I can't do. So will you think about it?"

"I'll think about it." He rolled closer and pulled her to him. "On the condition that for the next four days we do less talking and more of this." And when he kissed her and she kissed him back, nothing else mattered.

Blake pulled his car up to the sidewalk outside his apartment just as Bryn was leaving the building with his luggage. He opened the passenger window and leaned over. "I'll take you to the airport."

"No need." Bryn shoved a hand in his pocket and turned to look up the street. "I have an Uber coming."

Blake pressed the button for the trunk, got out, and moved to the pavement. "Get in the car, Bryn. We need to talk." Before his brother could argue, he picked up a piece of luggage and deposited it in the back of the car.

Bryn didn't move. "I've been waiting to talk to you for two whole days, Blake. What makes you think I'm going to suddenly jump when you click your fingers?"

"'Cause I have all your favorite shoes, and I'll drive off with them if you refuse." He tried a cheeky grin.

Bryn stared him down for a moment, then picked up another bag. "You'd better get me there on time."

"I've booked a flight for Tuesday," Blake said when Bryn had cancelled the Uber and they were moving through the traffic. "I'll fly into Salem to check out the retirement village, and then I'll hire a car and come see Mom and Dad."

Bryn stared out the side window. "Why the sudden change of heart? You doing an image job on yourself now?"

"No, I just realized I need to get this sorted."

"Realized? Or did someone call you out on your level of self-absorption and selfishness? I can guess who it was."

"Who said anything about Kirin?"

"I can't imagine you thought of this on your own," his brother said. "It was easy to see when I met her that you'd cast some sort of spell over her. She couldn't stop asking questions about you. I just hope you treat her well."

The comment stung, and Blake bit back the thought that, unlike his brother, at least he'd learned how to communicate with people. Now wasn't the time to have that conversation. In fact, he didn't want to make those sorts of judgments anymore.

Fixing things with his family was all down to Kirin, and that wasn't all she'd done for him. She'd made him want to be a better person in relationships, to take his time and enjoy things like the amazing food she'd cooked him. She'd called him out on the way he treated people sometimes, and she was the whole reason he was reconnecting with his twin after years of animosity.

Kirin Hart made him want to be a better man, and it was tearing him apart that she'd soon be gone.

He swallowed as the impact of not having her in his life

became real. She needed space to be the strong, independent woman she'd become. And that meant he needed to move on.

"My time with Kirin is up." He gripped the steering wheel as they hit the 10 freeway to the airport. "She has her career to focus on, and I'll be moving back to New York. We've achieved the goals we had for her, and she's moving on."

"So you'll both be focusing on your careers and pretending that's more important than anything else in life?"

His hands tightened on the wheel. "I think you and I are pretty even on that score," Blake said. "Maybe we're twins." He tried another grin and when he looked sideways his brother's mouth had curved a little. The tension holding his shoulders prisoner melted away.

"You've got a shot with someone pretty special there I'd say." Bryn still stared out the windscreen.

"No, Kirin and I are a short-term connection." Blake spoke to himself as much as to his brother, trying to convince both of them. "We both needed something from each other, and now that our contract is finished, we can move on. She's older than me and being associated with a younger guy, even when it was completely innocent, killed her reputation before. She's looking for something more than I can offer."

"Does she know that?" Surprise laced his brother's words.

"Of course she does, that's why she hired me. Soon she'll be starting a whole new life."

"It's a shame," Bryn said. "Maybe someone like Kirin could help you find more meaning in life."

Blake slapped a hand on the steering wheel. "I have

plenty of meaning in my life. By the end of next week I'll own the largest PR empire in the country, and I'm proud of that, even if members of my family aren't."

"We're proud enough. We just never get a chance to tell you."

They drove in silence for the next couple of miles, Blake wishing that Kirin was here to guide him. He hadn't said so many words to his brother since they were kids, and he didn't want it to end like this.

"And I'm proud of you, Bryn," he finally said. "More than proud. I'm honored to be your brother. When I'm working with a client, someone like Kirin, for example, someone who's lost confidence in what they can do, how they can use what they have to their best advantage, I often think of you. I know that what you achieve for people is life-changing, not just image-changing, but I like to think that a little bit of you is reflected in a little bit of me."

They stopped at traffic lights and Bryn turned to him. "I wouldn't underestimate what you do in terms of changing people's lives, Blake. If the confidence and passion I saw in Kirin is anything to go by. I'd say you're having an impact on people, too."

As he looked into the face of his brother for the first time in years, *really looked,* Blake recognized his own heart and it scared him to death. What he'd given Kirin made him the most proud he'd ever been in his life.

And he couldn't wait to tell her.

10

―――――

lthough she was racing around like a crazy person, getting ready for her big night tomorrow, Kirin wouldn't miss a day without chatting to Gwin and Ellie. They'd understand that she couldn't talk for long, but she wanted to come clean with them about where things were with her and Blake now. They'd been almost as much a part of her journey as Blake had these last couple of weeks, and she wanted to keep them in the loop. She clicked on the group chat.

Gwin: *Oh, you are here, K! We thought you might be too busy preparing for the big night tomorrow night.*

Kirin: *Things are hectic but I wanted to pop in and say that while I won't be around tomorrow night, I'll be carrying you two with me. I can't tell you guys how much your support has meant to me.*

Ellie: *You're so welcome and I'm so excited for you. What are you doing there?*

Ellie and Gwin knew Blake had arranged for her to be involved in a huge event that could really help in the resurrection of her career, but she hadn't told them exactly what she was going to do there.

A while back, when they'd discussed whether she should continue working with Blake given her feelings about him, Gwin had been very clear. She'd said that it was honesty and openness that defined the depth of a relationship. Now was her chance to be open and honest with them.

Kirin: *It's a charity dinner where a celebrity chef donates their time and hundreds of people pay exorbitant sums to eat their food.*

Ellie: *And you're organizing it? Dealing with the celebrity chef? Fancy?*

Kirin: *I . . .*

Gwin: *She is the celebrity chef. Aren't you, K?*

Kirin: *Wait, what? You knew who I was all along?!*

Gwin: *California's just a big old village when it comes down to it. Guessed you must be involved in something pretty huge when you mentioned you owned a company with a board in San Francisco. There's a design industry mag that I subscribe to and there was a story in there about what had happened to your brand and how you were getting back out there . . .*

Kirin: *And you didn't want to ask?*

Gwin: *I was DYING to ask!! But we have built our whole thing on sharing without fear or prejudice and I wanted you to still feel you could do that.*

Ellie: *I AM LOST!*

Kirin: *I'm going to tell you EVERYTHING when we meet next, E, I promise. For now, my real name is Kirin Hart and I can't tell you what the support of you two has meant for me. Now, quickly, tell me what's happening with the both of you so I can think about it instead of freaking out about cooking for 800 people?! Ellie, you first.*

Ellie: *Well, I'm back in Rata Cove and it's amazing. I'm* *swimming in the sea every morning, going for long walks on the beach, and the first public meeting is this coming weekend!! I know it's nothing like what you're facing tomorrow, Kirin, but I'm so nervous!!*

Kirin: *You'll absolutely smash it, Ellie. All of those people you knew as a kid will be blown away by what you're going to do for their little town.*

Ellie: *I really hope so. Gwin, what's happening with you?*

Gwin: *I'm sitting over here still star struck by the fact I know Kirin Hart!! My entire family used to watch your cooking shows and my mom's collecting labels from one of your soups for a competition right now!!!*

Kirin: *Oh, that's so cool!! But, the only thing I am is a fallen star and I'm hoping my performance tomorrow night doesn't turn me into a black hole.*

Gwin: *You'll have Blake there, right? Are things still simmering away with him (see what I did there . . !)*

Kirin: *I promise I'll fill you in on the Blake situation after the dinner. Right now, I want to know how your job applications are going, Gwin.*

Gwin: *I got one...*

Kirin: *WOOOHOOO!!!*

Gwin: *You're the first ones I've told. I'm so excited and scared and nervous that my sister will change her mind about wanting to come with me. It's an amazing opportunity but . . .*

Ellie: *I'm going to toast you both! Tonight when the sun goes down over the Tasman sea I'm going to toast you two amazing women.*

Kirin: *That's THE BEST news, Gwin!! And Ellie, when this dinner is over and you've had your first meeting and Gwin's told everyone she's moving to the city, why don't we have another toast - a face-to-face live toast on Skype or FaceTime or whatever. I don't care if it's in the morning for me, or the middle of the night,*

I just want to toast you two amazing women who've helped lift me up so high.
    Gwin: *I'm there!*
    Ellie: *CAN'T WAIT!!!*

***

Kirin stood at the entrance to the commercial kitchen of the Venice Ballroom the next evening as chefs finished cleaning up and waiters put the last of the empty dessert plates on the counter for the kitchen hands. She rubbed the back of a hand across her damp forehead as she walked down a curtained corridor and peeked into the enormous dining room. Just a few stragglers were finishing cheese platters, and others were deep in conversation over the last bottles of wine. The charity dinner had been an unprecedented success.

Her throat constricted and tears stung the back of her eyes. She was back. After a hellish year when she'd thought everything was lost, she was back where she belonged and it felt incredible. And she'd almost achieved this on her own. Blake had set this all up, of course, but she'd done the work and carried it through.

This time next week, when Dent and Douglas had approved her changes and Blake had bought the company, she would be on her own.

She knew she could do it. Knew that from here on in she was her own person, not a product, or a wife, or a part of a team. Kirin Hart~Solo—would be just that: Kirin without Blake. Without Blake in her business, in her bed, in her life. Her heart squeezed tight and tears threatened again, but she swiped them away. This was ending exactly as he'd promised her, with her image turned around and a whole new future to look forward to. He'd offered her nothing more, and she had no right to expect it.

In three days she would never see Blake again, and it was time to come to terms with it.

She dragged her attention back to the success of the night and lifted the microphone of her headset to her mouth, ready to congratulate Jacob, the maître d', for the incredible job he'd done.

Each course had gone out on time, perfectly coordinated with her cooking staff, and the compliments she'd heard from the guests were heart-warming. Jacob would be giving his staff their final clean up instructions, and she wanted to thank him before he left too. Then she'd report back to Jean-Pierre and her perfect night would be over.

"Jacob?" She adjusted her earpiece and static sounded over the airwaves. "Awesome job. I'd be honored to work with you again any time. I thought I'd get hung out to dry when people took so long getting back to their seats after the main, but you saved my butt."

"That perfect butt with the skin as smooth as whipped cream?"

She spun away from the curtain. "Blake?" She smiled at the sound of his rich, deep voice as she whispered into the microphone. "Get off this thing! Where's Jacob? Anyone could be listening."

"Not until you tell me how it feels to have catered the best event this venue's seen in years." His voice was sexy-low, and it sent sizzling heat down her spine. She'd hardly seen him since yesterday, and although she'd known he was in the background, helping to ensure everything went smoothly for her, she hadn't seen him all night. "Everyone raved about the food, Kirin. And you're a knockout in that dress." He dropped his voice to a whispered tease. "I'll overlook the fact it's not the one I told you to wear. But it's hot."

She tucked a strand of hair behind her ear, and warmth worked its way through her chest. "Where are you?" she whispered, taking another peek out the curtains.

"Close enough that I can see the dimple on your cheek." His voice was a low rumble in her ears. "And the glow on your face from when I talked about your ass."

She rubbed a hand across her neck as a cleaner walked past with a bucket and mop, and she grinned like a crazy woman.

"How does it feel to have pulled this off?" he asked.

This wasn't right. She wanted to see his face when she answered. Wanted him to see what all this meant for her. To know what he'd achieved. What they'd achieved *together*. She looked out across the room again, searching for his chestnut hair, his powerful body in a crisp dinner suit. She was desperate to see the smile she could hear in his voice. "Where are you?"

"Near enough to smell the perfume you put on this morning. Not quite close enough to kiss your neck."

Her nipples pearled at his dark and delicious tone. "Blake, what if Jacob hears us?"

"He won't. He took his headset off while he talks to his staff."

"I should go," she said, torn between listening to the voice that made her weak at the knees and finishing her job. "It's going to be a long night. I want to make sure every last pan is put away, every counter wiped down."

"Kirin." He sounded hesitant. "I wanted to say..." He cleared his throat. "I wanted to say how proud I am of everything you've achieved in the past two weeks."

She hadn't heard him like this before. Desperately, she searched across the room.

A movement from behind caused her to turn, and suddenly she found him standing in the shadows. Her stomach exploded in a flight of butterflies as his face broke into a broad grin.

In his arms. All she wanted was to be in his arms and pressing her lips on his mouth, on his throat, drinking him in. She crossed the gap between them, grabbed his hand, and dragged him further into the shadows. When they were stuck between a large column and a stainless steel trolley, she pulled him to her. "I want you now," she said, heat pulsing between her legs.

"I'll have you anytime, anywhere." He smiled into her cheek. "But shouldn't you sign off here?"

"I can make it quick…" She placed her hand in the center of his chest and pushed him back a fraction. "But unforgettable."

When he was an arm's length away, she dragged two fingers from his chest in a slow line to his belly button. "We never did get to lesson three. Far too much time spent practicing lessons one and two. We have a contract running out in three days, and I want to make sure my transformation is complete." She leaned in and whispered in his ear as her fingers trailed lower. "You wouldn't deny me lesson three?" Her hand dropped again until she felt the firm, rigid length of him through his fine suit pants.

That she could make him react like this thrilled her more than all the banquets she'd catered in her life. And the groan wrung deep from his throat as she stroked him which fired her on.

"Trouble is," she murmured, "once I start this sort of thing, I don't ever seem to be able to stop. Come with me."

She laced her fingers through his and led him past stacked boxes and opened the door of a storage cupboard.

Without switching the light on, she pushed him back in and kicked the door behind her. As soon as they were inside, his lips were on hers, his hands tangled through her hair.

"God, Kirin, you are beautiful, you smell beautiful." His hands slipped down to cradle her bottom. The light from under the door and the eerie glow from a refrigerator were all they had to see by. But Kirin didn't need light. Her fingers had explored Blake's chest often enough to know every muscle, every inch of skin. She pushed the jacket from his shoulders and let it drop to the floor, then undid the top few buttons of his shirt and raced her palms across his chest. While her hands explored the warm expanse, Blake claimed her mouth and kissed her as if she was oxygen.

"You don't know how much of a turn on it is to see you looking so hot and so in control," he said when he came up for breath.

"It's all down to you, Makeover Man." She spoke on a smile. "All of this is your creation. I'd say it's a job well done."

He swept his hand down her back and pulled her to him while she struggled to unlatch his belt. Hot and hard, he kissed her mouth 'til his fingers joined hers and together they undid his trousers. Wanting every scrap of him she could lay claim to, Kirin pushed the cotton boxers down and took his shaft in her hand. The pulsing need within him radiated through her palm, and she dropped to her knees.

Blake slammed his palm on the wall in front of him as Kirin knelt and took him in her mouth. Her lush lips closed around his length, and he groaned out her name. The fantasy of taking her in a public place was trumped a thousand times by the reality of her expertly giving him pleasure. Gently, she cupped his balls, her tongue and lips still working their magic, and he sucked air through his teeth. He was going to explode soon, and there was nowhere he wanted to do that more than deep inside Kirin, with the scent of her hair in his nose and the feel of her body under his fingers.

"Come here, baby, come here," he said as he reached for her.

A sound of protest came from her throat. But he knew he was close and wasn't going to miss the full power of them making love together.

He touched her shoulders, and she moved up his body, licking his stomach and then laying a kiss by his mouth.

"Panties off," he growled and lifted the skirt of her dress till he found the edge of her panties and then his fingers stilled. Lightly, he brushed across the front of her and she moaned. "Lace. These are lace," he said, smiling. "And I can't even see them."

She let out a laugh, then peeled them off.

He lifted her until she was pinned against the wall; her legs around his waist and his erection nudged her entrance. "We don't have protection," he groaned.

"Oh, God," she moaned. "Now, Blake, now, please. I went back on the pill. I can't wait."

She was wet, and he was beyond ready, and in one swift thrust, he was inside her. Strands of her silky hair teased the skin across his shoulders as he thrust with more urgency. Deeper and deeper he pushed into her, and each time her muscles welcomed him with a tight embrace.

If only he could see her eyes, the sparkle he'd witnessed so many times when she was about to come, the way her lids fluttered and her mouth pursed as she reached her peak. This time it was the sound she made that told him she was near, and then she called his name, at first as a whisper and then louder and louder until he smothered his name on her lips and together they traveled up and over the edge.

He put his face to her cheek. It was damp. "Are you okay? Are you crying?"

"Of course not." She lifted her face from his and cleared her throat. "Perspiration from over-exerting myself."

He dipped his head to her shoulder and stayed still for a moment, paying reverence to all she'd just given him. And then he unhooked her legs from his waist and eased her to the floor.

"Whoa," she said, and in the dim light he saw her pulling on her panties and straightened her dress. "That's more invigorating than the after-dinner mint I was planning to eat."

He laughed as she pulled his shirt back on his shoulders and helped him with his buckle. "Come back to my place tonight," he said. "We only have two more days before your TV interview, and there are a few things we should go over."

"We can meet Sunday, or even early Monday morning." She was doing up his buttons. "I might get nervous if I do too much planning."

"What about lesson four?" He held her wrists still, wishing he could look in her eyes and read what was going on in her head, see why her voice was changing.

"Is there a lesson four?" she said. "Or are you making this up as you go along?"

"There can be a lesson four if you want there to be." He cupped a breast through the fabric of her dress. "And you should know me well enough by now to understand that I don't make things up as I go along."

"I think a weekend apart might do us good." Her voice was light and breezy. Too breezy and distant. "Why don't we meet for breakfast before we go to the studio Monday, and you can talk me through the things I should say and not say. Then when it's all over, and providing it's gone well, maybe we can have a drink to celebrate before you go back to New York."

This was it. Kirin didn't need him anymore. And why would she? Her career was back on track, her picture with her new sexy image was showing up daily in the newspapers. And if what she'd just done to him against the wall of a storage cupboard was anything to go by, she'd got her sexual mojo back and then some. Kirin Hart didn't need him anymore, and it hurt like hell.

"And try not to let them steer the conversation back to the old days." Blake leaned beside Kirin at her kitchen counter Monday morning, his dark green eyes hooded as he watched her putting on make-up.

All the powders and pencils Pippa had taught her to master were now being put to use as she dabbed her nose, then combed her newly groomed and colored brows. The makeup artist on the show would do a touch-up job, but she wanted to arrive looking her best.

And she was looking better than the puffy-eyed vision she'd woken to the past two mornings. She wasn't ashamed to admit she'd cried through the weekend, just as she'd cried the last time she'd made love with Blake. This was all part of shedding her old, vulnerable self, and she was getting used to how much it hurt.

"This will be the turning point, Kirin. It's your first exposure back on national television, the first chance to talk about the future, and your first opportunity to show off everything we've achieved in the last two weeks." He bent and scratched Dudley behind the ears, and her dog threw himself unceremoniously at Blake's feet.

Kirin rubbed her lips together, then sat back on the stool. "What if I screw up? What if Felicity does what Larry Williams did and throws me something like a sex tape?"

He reached out and took her hand, stroking the sensitive skin on the inside of her wrist. And her blood heated. "Then you'll do what we practiced. You'll rise above it, project all the confidence we know is inside you, and you'll say that private lives are private and you're not prepared to talk about it. But that you are prepared to talk about your new ice cream brand or the charity dinner."

He looked so confident, so sure she could pull this off, and her chest tightened. When she'd met Blake, she'd wanted to succeed for herself. Prove to everyone around her that she was a good person, a great businesswoman, and an excellent cook who'd never use her power over an employee. Now, looking at this man who'd touched her on levels she never knew existed, the only person she wanted to do this for was him.

She wanted Blake to be proud of her—not just in the way she looked, but the way she spoke, what she stood for, what she wanted to be. What she'd achieved as a woman and a businesswoman. She'd spent the better part of the weekend fighting the urge to call and tell him she couldn't sleep without him holding her, couldn't cook without him asking why parmesan smelled of old socks, and hearing his groan as he watched her pull on leggings or put her hair in a scrunchie.

But that wasn't part of the deal anymore. After today, Blake's job would be done, and she'd be on her own again. She could do it, she'd come to know herself in these past few weeks like she'd never imagined. What she hadn't counted on was falling in love with Blake.

Falling in love?

She gripped the makeup brush until it dug into her palm. She loved him. The thought ran wild in her head, and her pulse drummed at her temple, the complicated, impossible knowledge racing through her blood.

He was still speaking to her, caressing her wrist with no understanding of the monumental revelation, no knowledge of how he'd slipped into her heart and would never leave it.

And he never would know.

She needed to move on, to be a strong and independent woman or he wouldn't get the thing he wanted most in life —the biggest PR empire in the country. With shaking fingers, she drew back and tucked a strand of hair behind her ear. Burying her feelings for him.

For now.

"There's a studio audience this time. That makes me way more nervous than before. See, I'm trembling already."

He folded his arms across his chest. "You've been in front of a camera more times than most of these people have had hot dinners. You're a professional, you know the drill, and you're going to be fine. And besides, I'll be there." Complicated emotions swam in his eyes.

She twisted to look at him. "You'll be there?" The pulse in her temple became a dull, hard ache. She wouldn't be able to concentrate on anything when they were together in public. It made her think back to the storeroom and the heights he'd taken her to.

"There's a live studio audience so there's no reason for me not to be there. And besides, I can't wait to see people's reactions when they watch you and hear you." He smiled tenderly. "You're going to blow them away."

Terror gripped her insides. What if people could tell she was in love? In her current state, she wasn't sure she wouldn't screw everything up completely. "What if I choke? What if they throw something at me I'm not expecting?"

He dropped his tone to sexy smooth and his mouth hitched. "You think there might've been a security camera in the storeroom? That really would have made lesson three public."

When she gasped, he took her hand and pulled her to her feet while Dudley lumbered away. "Kirin, stop worrying. You look sensational, you *are* sensational. You'll have everyone eating out of your hands, and you won't even remember these past two weeks soon. You'll be inundated with TV appearances and endorsements. I've spoken to your publicist, and he's told them which subjects to avoid. We've said you'll make one brief comment about the sexual harassment suit but that it's not going to be the focus of the interview."

She bit her lip and looked up at him. "Whatever happens, I want you to know how grateful I am for everything you've done for me."

He put a finger to her lips, then bent his head and covered her mouth with his. For what could be their last moments together, Kirin melted into him, savoring his strength, his confidence and his never-ending belief in her. A deep, shaking sob built from the deepest part of her, but she smothered it dead.

"No more talk," he said, when he finally drew his lips away. "This is the moment when the new Kirin Hart is launched on the world. Go get 'em".

Two hours later, studio lights burned to the back of Kirin's eyes, and her makeup felt as if it might melt and slide down her cheeks. It was too late to run and hide. The opening credit music was playing in her ear, and Felicity Farrell, the show's host, was giving her the final nod, indicating they were about to go live.

Her heart galloped. Everything hinged on what she said now—the public's view of her past, her future, Blake's future. In one last going-to-the-gallows movement, she let her eyes drift to the audience. They were shadowed in darkness, a sea of nameless faces, except for one she was so desperate to see right now. Where was Blake?

The floor manager began clapping, and the audience joined in. With memories of her last live TV appearance rolling through her mind, her stomach did a half-pike double twist.

" . . . and my very special guest today is the celebrity chef and homemaking mogul, Kirin Hart. Welcome, Kirin. It feels like a long time since your fans have seen you in public." Felicity gave a sweet smile. "How have things been for you lately?"

She shifted on the chair, suddenly aware of how short the skirt was that Blake had picked out for her. Was she showing too much leg? Not enough? Should she cross her ankles? Sit sideways, or look straight into the camera?

"Thanks so much for having me, Felicity." Her mouth

dried, the words sticking to her tongue. "It's been a while, but it's lovely to be back."

Felicity's voice lowered. "Let's talk a little about that sexual harassment suit."

Straight for the jugular.

Kirin squeezed her hands together on her lap. "I'm afraid that for legal reasons, I can't speak about any details to do with the suit, Felicity. What I can say is I'm very happy to be moving forward with my life after a very tough couple of years." She moved her mouth to smile and, to her horror, realized her lips were trembling.

"Moving forward? In what way?"

She breathed a little slower. "I have a great new ice cream brand that we'll be launching in the summer, I'm back doing guest catering—I just cooked for eight hundred people at the Venice Ballroom—and I'm in talks with a TV production company about a new cooking show."

"Sounds fantastic, Kirin. We all love your down home style and the real..." She paused. "Honesty you bring to your brand. And is your whole new look a part of these projects or is there another reason for your makeover?" Felicity turned toward the camera more. "You don't mind my mentioning the fact that your appearance has undergone quite a dramatic transformation in the last couple weeks?"

A chill worked its way down her spine. "I guess it's always a good idea to freshen things up."

Felicity raised an eyebrow. "So your funky new skirts and high heels have nothing to do with having a new man? A younger man in your life."

Unbidden, her eyes swung out to the audience as her heart began to pound. How did they know? Who'd let this leak? Colin? Alex? Her mom? God, if people knew what had been happening with Blake, not only would she and her brand be back to square one, but Blake's takeover of D and D would be on the line too.

"I, ah..." Sweat trickled down her back.

"Rumor has it that he's had a very big influence on this whole fresh look of yours and that the two of you have become ... extremely close."

Suddenly, her eyes landed on Blake, and it felt as if the whole world knew what she was thinking. He sat perfectly still, his rugged features composed to relaxed calm.

A pulse beat sharp in her throat, and she tried to swallow it away. There were two possible answers to that question. She could deny Blake's existence, say this was all her own work, that she was now strong and free and independent and ready to take on the world. Or she could say yes, a younger man has had an influence on her, and due to his guidance and support she was now strong and free and ready to take on the world.

One of those answers was a lie, and she was sick to death of lying.

"I don't believe any woman should be judged by the relationships she has, Felicity. I've worked too hard over the course of my career to be judged by what happens in my personal life. But having said that, yes, I have been influenced by a man who came in to my life to help me with my image and I'll be forever in his debt."

"But your *personal* life—with Joe Hart—was so much of what made you successful. You must understand that your fans feel a loyalty to Joe and everything he stood for as well. How are they supposed to trust this whole new image of you, *and* a new relationship, after everything that's happened since Joe died?"

She was referring to what she had with Blake as a new relationship. God, how had they gotten wind of this? "I do understand that, but I'd also hope my fans would want me to be happy, and they'd be more interested in my food than what I wore or who I was dating." The words had fallen from her mouth before she'd really thought them through.

Felicity leaned forward, little bubbles of saliva forming at the corner of her mouth. "What a lot of us are really asking is, will the real Kirin Hart please stand up? Perhaps you can show her to us after the commercial break."

Suddenly people were moving across the stage again. A woman came to powder Kirin's nose and Felicity was joking with the floor manager about the next guest. All Kirin wanted to do was get the hell out of the hole she was digging herself into. She looked out at the studio audience to see Blake chatting to the women on either side of him.

Who was the real Kirin Hart? Was she the woman Blake had been so desperate to transform? The one who'd had no sense of herself and no idea how to be sexy? Or was she the woman who, once transformed with the help of Blake's skill and attention, suddenly became someone he wanted to have in his bed? Had she become Frankenstein's monster, someone who fell in love with her creator but someone who that creator would never truly know?

She watched as the women giggled and twirled their hair and how Blake seemed to come alive with their attention, and something shifted inside her. She knew the answers to Felicity's questions, and she also knew that she'd lived a lie for the greater part of her life. The nightmare of the harassment suit would be played out over and over if she continued to cover her real feelings. If she wanted to show the world that she was a whole new person, then she wanted to start with the truth.

~

Blake watched Kirin under the studio lights and his chest filled with pride. She looked stunning in her tight black skirt, high heels, and flowing blouse. Her hair fanned rich and blond around her shoulders, and she'd applied her makeup perfectly. It was interesting that he'd been implicated in her makeover and the hint that he and Kirin were together, but he was sure she'd handle that fine in the next segment. Just fifteen minutes more and he'd have pulled off one of the greatest image turnarounds in history.

"Welcome back," Felicity Farrell was saying. "Today we're talking to Kirin Hart, one-time member of the hugely successful 'Cooking with Hart' husband and wife celebrity chef team, and now a woman bravely going solo after the untimely death of her husband."

Felicity swiveled towards Kirin, a 'going for the kill' look on her face. "Kirin, you were about to tell us which of the Kirin Harts we've seen is the real one. The wholesome, dependable woman we saw as part of the 'Cooking with Hart' partnership, or this bombshell we have in front of us now."

Kirin dipped her chin, and Blake smiled in anticipation of what she'd say. She'd talk about how free she felt now, how embracing her authentic, sexy, feminine side had finally set her on the path of change and enlightenment. He could just imagine what she was about to say becoming sound bites in the papers and entertainment shows tomorrow.

"I'm neither of those two people," Kirin said as she raised her face. "Both of those looks were designed by someone else for a commercial reason, and if I'm to tell you the truth then I really don't know who I am."

His blood ran cold. What in the hell was she doing?

Sensing a tangent to this story that she wasn't expecting,

or perhaps blood she'd inadvertently let, Felicity leaned forward. "You mean you've been influenced by others and what they expect you to act and look like?"

"That's right. Just as so many women do in their lives and jobs, I struggle with who I am and how I should present myself. Always have, and probably always will. But I've realized I'm okay with that."

Blake's fingers curled around the armrests of his seat. This wasn't what they'd rehearsed. If she said all the right things now, she could have everything she wanted—a fresh new image and a whole new level of success for her business.

He leaned forward, hungering to hear more.

"So, you feel you've been easily influenced in your career?"

Kirin crossed her legs. "That's exactly what I mean, Felicity. Being a successful chef has been an incredibly rewarding life, but it's also been extremely hard work. And sometimes within that hard work it's easy to lose sight of what really matters."

Blake watched the people in the audience as they moved forward in their seats. They were captivated by Kirin. Not by her clothes or her new hairdo, but by the increasing passion in her voice.

"I've learned a whole lot of things in just two short weeks," she said with certainty. "I've learned that you can't choose who you fall in love with, that sometimes it's not the right person at the right time, but that you need to acknowledge it, embrace it, and move on. I've learned that people can protect their deepest hearts for fear of being hurt by those they love, but that you can't fully open yourself to love until you learn to love yourself."

His phone buzzed in his pocket and he took it out and

threw a look at the screen. The CEO of Dent and Douglas was calling, and Blake knew exactly what he was going to say, but for a surreal second he didn't care. All he cared about was watching Kirin and listening to the things that were coming from her heart. He switched the phone off and turned his gaze back to her. How had he not seen any of this coming?

"Hang on a minute." Felicity was nearly falling from her chair in a bid to get her next question out. "You're in *love* with the man who created this new image for you?"

Kirin's chest moved up and down. "That's right, but as I said, Felicity, I don't believe any woman should be judged by her relationships. What I *do* believe is that the real me isn't fancy clothes and gorgeous shoes. I'm just a woman who wants to cook food that people love, to enjoy the togetherness of friends and family, and to be around people who love me for me."

Blake froze. Loved? He pulled in a breath as his heart slammed against his ribcage. The shock of hearing her so open about her fears and insecurities had been one thing, but to find out along with the rest of the world that . . . she loved him?

The three words reeled through his mind, and he stared at the stage in disbelief. His lungs squeezed tight as he watched Kirin blink under the studio lights—that beautiful woman who wore her heart so courageously on her sleeve.

If she loved him, she'd be right back at square one, and so would he.

And if he loved her?

His throat closed. The desire to be with her every second of every day warred with his dream to see this project through, to reach the pinnacle he'd dreamed of so long.

And then words she'd said a moment ago came

tumbling back at him. Sometimes it's not the right person at the right time. *Sometimes you need to embrace it and move on.* And his heart stopped.

A woman in front of him started to clap, and then the person next to her joined in, until the entire audience was applauding and rising to their feet.

Kirin looked startled, as if she'd said those things to herself, not to an audience of thousands. She didn't smile, didn't acknowledge the people around her, she just sat staring into the camera and Blake knew he couldn't get to her quickly enough.

11

"I don't understand." Blake spoke quietly as he leaned against the wall of the green room and scrubbed a hand across his chin fifteen minutes later. Kirin sat slumped in a hard wooden chair opposite, her heart still thumping, tears threatening at the thought of what she'd done.

She loved Blake Matthews, and that was bad enough. To have made that declaration for the very first time on live national television was unconscionable. And given the opportunity, she'd do it all over again.

"After we'd planned so carefully what you'd talk about, I've got to say I was pretty taken aback by some of your revelations." His tone was cautious, defensive even, and of course she couldn't blame him for it. His face was a mask.

She stared straight ahead, a sour mix of sadness, horror, and relief rolling through her. He began to speak again, but she cut him off. "Of course you were." She turned to face him and lifted her chin. "But after everything I've learned in the last couple of weeks, I have to tell the truth from now on, Blake, to my family and friends, and to my fans. I'm just so sorry that my honesty will mean you won't get what you want. I know you and I can never be together. I'm the last person you can be seen with now I've destroyed things between you and Dent and Douglas, but I had to say those things tonight. I don't want to bury my true self so deep that I don't know where to find it, and I'm not going to live like that anymore."

He dug a hand through his hair. "I'm so proud of everything you've achieved and the way the audience reacted to your honesty today. I want you to know that whatever happens from now with your career and with D and D, I'll have no regrets when we move on."

There was something different about him, a distance that she hadn't seen since the first time they'd met, and she ached for the real Blake to speak to her. Had she killed even their friendship by declaring her love for him publicly?

She took a steadying breath as she tried to stop the tremble in her lips and failed. She'd expected this reaction, of course she had, but it didn't lessen the crack in her heart that their time together was ending, with neither of them getting what they wanted. "I love the things you've taught me, Blake, the way you've encouraged me. I value those things more than you'll ever know. I just hope you can learn to let more people see the incredible parts of you that I've seen."

He swung around and stared at her, eyes turning deep sea green. "What do you mean?"

"You hide behind your looks, Blake. You make them an excuse for being aloof, for not opening your heart, and letting people see what's inside. But I *know* what's in there. I've seen it when we're together, when we make love, when you're about to go over the edge, you open yourself up and it's beautiful. You've changed my life completely and I love you. I will not lie about that."

He nodded slowly, still not acknowledging that she'd said she loved him. But they were her feelings, not his. "You're right. I've never been good at looking inside. Holding a mirror up to other people is a hell of a lot easier. You've got all the skills you need to present your strong, independent self to the world. You don't need D and D or me anymore. Now is your time to shine on your own."

From within her deepest heart she wanted to make Blake understand not only what he meant to her, but why she'd declared her love and why she had to let him go.

"You held a mirror up to me and made me look so very hard at myself. At first I didn't want to acknowledge I'd been denying my authentic self for so long, but you challenged me, pushed me to learn to love myself." She struggled for a deeper breath. "What I was hoping you'd do in that time is hold that same mirror up to yourself so you could see deep inside, too. But you didn't, and I don't think you ever will, and that breaks my heart more than you'll ever know."

"I never offered you anything more," Blake said. "We agreed that we'd go our separate ways when our time was up, and now that you've re-established yourself in your own way, that's more important than ever."

Her lips trembled as a wave of sadness threatened to overtake her. He wasn't listening, would never listen. There was nothing more to say.

She stood and hugged herself for fear of falling apart in front of him. "Goodbye, Blake. I'm truly sorry you're going to lose your chance with D and D, but I'll never forget you. Good luck with your business and your family." As the tears blinded her eyes, she straightened her back and walked from the room.

~

Five days later, Blake let himself into his San Francisco apartment for what would probably be the final time. He'd left for Oregon after the Felicity Farrell interview, primarily because he had tickets booked, but also because he sensed Kirin needed time on her own. He'd been floored by her declaration and thrown when she'd said the time wasn't right for them. One second he'd been walking on air, the next crushed by the realization he'd fallen short for her in every area.

Spending time with Bryn and his parents had been a lot more pleasant than he'd imagined, and they'd made some progress for his parents' future. But now he needed to pack and get back to New York.

Oregon had been a good place to escape from the paparazzi and the phone calls, too. There were over a dozen voice messages from D and D, but he hadn't listened to any of them. He'd deal with that tomorrow when he went in to their offices to face the fallout from his failed buyout.

He hoped Kirin hadn't had to deal with all the phone calls and photographers, too. He'd employed some private security to secretly protect her house from the press, but they'd reported that she hadn't been staying there. She hadn't returned any of his calls either, and it was starting to get to him. Not that he could blame her. She'd told him she loved him, and he'd left her hanging.

He couldn't get her out of his head. It wasn't surprising given they'd spent so much time together in the past two weeks, or the way things ended between them. But it was more than that. He thought about her when he first woke, when he was falling asleep, and every second in between. Even his dreams were filled with the memory of her smile and the feel of her body under his. Her silky hair across his chest, her passion for food and feeding him, of waking up with a smile on his face, knowing he was going to see her.

He walked to his bedroom, the apartment's cold and clinical decoration irritating him. He'd missed Kirin's warm and inviting home and the enigmatic Dudley way too much. Some mornings he'd tried to remember how she'd looked, standing at his stove cooking, the cheeky smile she'd give him when he'd steal a kiss.

He tossed his luggage on the floor, then bone weary, threw himself on the bed. Kirin's final words to him had been on shuffle in his head. I was hoping you'd hold a mirror up to yourself so you could see deep inside. *But you didn't.*

And then memories of the way he'd felt in her arms came flooding back. She'd pushed him to address his issues with Bryn, challenged him to make amends with his family. She'd called him out on his time management and the way he abused his body with food.

An iron hand fisted tight in his chest.

He hadn't held a mirror up to himself. *She had.*

Kirin was his mirror. She'd stood in front of him and reflected what was deep inside and he'd let her. She'd accepted his distance and his barriers, but she'd pushed beyond them, slipping under his skin without him even knowing it was happening. And it had changed his life. Had changed him.

From somewhere deeply buried, a frightening and impossible thought overtook him. He'd never see her again, would never again be inside the world of Kirin Hart and the honesty she brought to his life. The realization chilled him to the bone.

He got off the bed and rifled through the things on his

bedside table. When he didn't find what he was looking for, he raced to the lounge room and pushed aside papers on the coffee table. There it was.

He held up the photo he'd taken when she'd come to show him the new dress she'd picked out. She was radiant— so different to the closed and defensive woman he'd met that very first day.

In this picture she was so full of confidence and positivity and...

Something cracked within his chest. What had made Kirin's smile wider and her eyes shine brighter in this shot? It hadn't been him and his designer dresses and slick haircuts. It had been because Kirin had opened her heart to something new and challenging. With honesty and optimism and faith, she'd opened her heart and from that second forward, she'd blossomed.

If she could do that, then why couldn't he?

His chest swelled as a new realization bloomed inside him. There was something he had to tell Kirin Hart, something so huge and so frightening that if he didn't go now, he might never have the guts. He picked up his wallet and keys and strode out the door.

Kirin sprinkled fresh cilantro over the vegetable curry she'd just made and wiped her hands on her apron. Cooking in other people's kitchens was always a challenge, but it was so lovely of Lucy to invite her to stay until the media circus died down. Not much chance of that happening any time soon.

In the last five days her face had appeared in newspapers, on the TV, You Tube, Instagram, Twitter and in online celebrity gossip columns. She hadn't seen all of it, but Lucy reported that it had all been incredibly positive. Seemed her fans had been touched by her honesty and openness, and even the CEO of Dent and Douglas admitted they were delighted by the city's change of heart towards her. Despite it being the result she'd wanted from the very beginning of her transformation, now she wanted so much more. Blake.

At least he'd get his company after all.

Lucy would be home soon, and they'd eat curry, drink beer, and watch a romantic comedy until they were laughing or crying, or both. The opportunity to cry in public was a relief. Since Blake had left, she hadn't let herself do it in private. There was such a deep, gaping hole inside her that she didn't know if she could stop once she started, but letting a little out in public at just the right moment seemed to help.

There was a knock at the door and Dudley lifted his head from his chopped steak and trotted down the hallway. Strange that Lucy hadn't let herself in with a key, and equally strange that Dudley hadn't barked if it wasn't Lucy.

She followed her dog to the door and looked through the peephole to be sure there wasn't a crowd of journalists or photographers. Seeing no one and nothing there, she put on the security chain and opened the door a fraction.

A cardboard box sat on the welcome mat with no one in sight. She opened the door, retrieved the package, and stepped back inside.

It was wrapped in badly creased brown paper with a piece of old string around it. Should she open it? Maybe it was a hoax? Some radio show prank. She put it on the floor and studied it.

Dudley sniffed all around the box and then lay in a heap beside it and whined.

Too impatient to look for scissors, she pulled back the string and the paper slipped off. She undid the tape at the top and pulled out the straw-like packing material. When she saw what was inside, her heart missed a beat and tears welled.

With a trembling lip, she pulled out a porcelain pepper shaker in the shape of Rhett Butler from Gone with the Wind. She held the cool object in shaking fingers and bit her lip. Her mom wouldn't do this, would she? It had to be from Blake. Was it a peace offering? A final acknowledgement of the time they'd had together? She drew her finger over the image of Rhett, black suited, and on his knee. She couldn't wait to reunite him with Scarlett.

Looking back into the box, she found a small white envelope and opened it. "Meant to be together."

Tears fogged her eyes, and she laughed out loud just as there was another knock on the door. He'd be back in town to get the rest of his things, to make his peace and move on from her once and for all. It was going to be the hardest thing she'd ever done, but she'd shake his hand, thank him for everything, and wish him all the best.

She took a steadying breath, tacked on a smile, and opened the door.

The sight of Blake leaning against the doorjamb sent a wave of pain through her body. His chestnut hair was a little disheveled, the stubble at his chin more rugged than usual, and there was a wildness in his eyes she'd never seen before.

"Can I come in?" he said, and she nodded as she let him past. "I'm sorry but I had to ask your mom where I could find you when you weren't at home."

"That's okay. Thank you for Rhett. Scarlett's going to be so happy."

"You don't know how many online stores I've scoured

trying to track him down." There was a soft smile on his achingly handsome face. "Then I had to call Lucy to find out where you were."

They'd reached the kitchen and Kirin placed Rhett on the counter and moved behind it, her palms damp and her throat tight. "Would you like a drink?" She gave Dudley a pat as he resumed his steak dinner. "I guess you're back to pack your things before you head to New York. You left a jacket and pair of pants at my place but I didn't bring them here, sorry. I'll send them on. You must be pleased D and D were so happy with the publicity since the interview."

He frowned and shook his head. "I haven't spoken to anyone since the interview, and I don't want to talk about work. Come here, Kirin." His eyes were soft, his hands set low on his hips.

She bit her lip as her pulse beat hard in her throat, but stayed where she was. She didn't want any analysis; him feeling sorry for her or telling her that he'd think of her sometimes. Every part of her ached for him, and it was almost too much to bear.

"Okay, then, I'll come to you."

He moved into the kitchen and the memory of them making love on a counter top sent a stab to her throat. She missed him with a pain that ripped through her. This was too much, he was too close, and the tears she'd saved for the rom-com threatened to spill.

"We're good," she said hurriedly. "Really, I…"

"I have some things I want to say." Blake took her hand and, eyes locked on hers, lifted it to his lips. He placed a kiss on her palm. "I've found the mirror."

She frowned, too busy focusing on the tingle floating from her palm to her arm to make sense of what he meant. "In the shop where you found Rhett?"

He smiled. "You're my mirror, Kirin."

She swallowed and drew her hand back. "We don't need to do this, Blake. It was over before it started and I always knew that it would be. We don't need to go over it again."

He leaned in and, with the lightest, most sensual movement, brushed his lips against hers. Her eyes fluttered, and she held her breath, but as soon as he drew back she went on full alert.

"You said something to me the last time we were together, and I've been trying to get my head around it ever since."

Her heart raced, but she focused on his mouth and his words.

"I *have* held a mirror up to myself, Kirin, and it's you. Despite me being the most stubborn-assed, self-centered guy in the world, when I'm with you I can see the real me and although at first I didn't like what I saw, I've realized I want to make it happen over and over again. You and I have looked in a hundred mirrors together, but I haven't seen anything as clearly as when I'm with you. You make me want to be a better person, and I'll fight with everything inside myself to have you in my life. I want to be with you."

She pulled in a sharp breath and stepped away from him. "No, Blake. You don't need me and you don't like celebrities. You have a family who loves you, a business you're proud of, and any woman in the world would be lucky to have you."

"I don't want *any* woman, Kirin. I want you. Celebrity or otherwise. And not for two weeks or two months, or two years. I want to be with you every single minute of every single day and night forever, and I'm hoping like hell that you want me, too."

She shook her head, desperate to believe his words,

willing everything he said to come from his heart. But how could she be sure?

He moved closer. "We've achieved an incredible amount together in the last few weeks, from the way you dress, to the way you carry yourself. But those aren't the things I love about you, Kirin. It's not a dress that you've worn, or a shoe that you've modeled. It's not a haircut or the way you curl your lashes. Those aren't the things I love about you."

She locked her knees together to keep from falling, but she concentrated on his perfect face and let his words wash over her.

"I love you because you own the ugliest dog I've ever seen and yet you treat him like a prince. And you didn't name him Kujo or Brutus, you named him Dudley, and it couldn't suit him better."

He took her hand in his and the private tears she'd locked down tight pushed to the surface and spilled over. "I love you because, not only do you have a crazy condiment collection, but you're so proud of it you put it on display. It says so much about who you are and what you believe that it makes me want to believe it too. Kirin, I want to be the pepper to your salt, the lime to your tequila, the herb to your groundhog."

She squeezed his hand as she started to laugh, but he kept on talking.

"I love you because, despite the fact you've been made over and under, upside down and back to front, you'll still go to the grocery store in your gray leggings and alligator clip, regardless of who's watching, and you look stunning. I love you because you love your mom, even though she stresses you out. I love you because you make and keep friends and you push people to be the best they can be. Most of all I love you for your open heart, and because after watching you achieve all those things in your life, it made me want to achieve them, too."

"Oh, Blake." He opened his arms, and she stepped into them. "I haven't been able to imagine not seeing you, not touching you, not sharing my days with you."

He bent his head, and this time his kiss was strong and firm and sure and without a doubt in her heart. She believed everything he said. Their breaths mingled as the kiss deepened and Blake wrapped his arms around her.

When Dudley whined because the kiss had gone on for so long, Kirin tipped her head back and looked at Blake. "But what about D and D and your business and mine and the age gap and—"

Blake put a finger to her lips and smiled. "You know what I think will solve all our problems?"

She shook her head and hooked her hands behind his neck. "What?"

"I reckon that with a bowl of that cheese gnocchi and a night of making love, you and I can solve anything."

When he leaned in and kissed her again, Kirin knew he was absolutely right.

Thank you so much for reading **Bad Reputations**. I hope you love Kirin and Blake as much as I do! If you'd like to find out when Book 2 in the series releases, and receive a **FREE** prequel to the **Tall, Dark and Driven series,** *Waiting on Forever—Alex's story*, sign up to my newsletter here.

Find out what's happening for the characters of Brentwood Bay in the *Tall, Dark and Driven* series! You can find Book 1,

Making the Love List—Yasmin's story as an ebook on Amazon here, or ask for it at your local bookstore or library.

I hugely appreciate your help in spreading the word about my books, including telling a friend. Reviews help readers find books! Please review **Bad Reputations here** or on your favorite site.

Turn the page for the blurb and an excerpt from Book 2 in **The Breaking Through series,** *Desperate Measures ~ Ellie's story*

NEXT IN THE BREAKING THROUGH SERIES

DESPERATE MEASURES ~ ELLIE'S STORY

A wife he needs. The woman he desires.

Cy Hathaway needs a wife, fast, to win custody of his son, Jonty. He returns to New Zealand to discover the childhood sweetheart he once left behind has become a vibrant, beautiful woman. Even though wanting to sweep her off her feet wasn't part of the plan...

For Ellie, Cy's sudden reappearance awakens a flood of memories—and resentments for the way he'd abandoned her all those years ago. But she has a life now, a career. She can't simply drop everything and get hitched, even if the sight of him still makes her heart race.

But after Ellie meets his little boy, she can't refuse. Certain she has a grip on her old feelings for Cy, she agrees to marry her first love until he gains custody. But when did helping out a friend become something with the capacity to hijack her heart?

Turn the page to read Chapter One of *Desperate Measures ~ Ellie's story.*

You can preorder *Desperate Measures ~ Ellie's story* here.

DESPERATE MEASURES ~ ELLIE'S STORY
CHAPTER ONE

With the sun of a New Zealand summer's day burning through his black T-shirt, Cy Hathaway bent and peered in the old hall window. He scrubbed the heel of his hand across a fine film of dust and cobwebs, screwed one eye shut, and peered in with the other.

Rows of people in shorts and T-shirts sat on wooden benches, listening intently to the presentation. His heart drummed deep in his chest, jet lag and the anticipation of what he was about to do scrambling his thoughts. It wasn't the meeting that had drawn him to this hall from the other side of the world. It was the speaker, Ellie Jacobs. A girl from his past, someone he hadn't seen in eight years. And if everything went according to his carefully constructed plan, the woman who'd soon be his stand-in wife.

Despite this being the longest shot known to humankind—and the most selfish thing he'd ever asked—he couldn't leave New Zealand until she agreed to marry him. He'd managed to get the grandparents to give him two weeks with his son over Christmas, but after that . . .

Ellie Jacobs was his last chance.

If only she could forgive him for everything he'd done.

He pushed open the heavy door and a crowd of bodies twisted as one on their regulation wooden benches. The hall hadn't changed since he'd left as a teenager. Dust motes shimmied in the air, and the place still smelled of hot sun on polished wood. Red and green Christmas decorations trailed haphazardly from the ceiling, and the portrait of a young Queen Elizabeth hung crooked on the wall.

"I'll be staying at Starfish Cottage, if anyone has more questions in the next few . . ." The lyrical voice from the front faded to nothing.

"Hi." He lifted a hand and his words echoed in the quiet corners of the hall. "Sorry I'm late. Holiday traffic, and I forgot what these country roads can be like. Hoped I'd get here earlier."

There were murmured hellos and the man next to him stood, his blue eyes twinkling under bushy brows. "Cy, great to see you. It's been a long time, son."

He smiled and took Jack Parker's extended hand, but his gaze was glued to the lectern. Was that Ellie? That stunning woman in black trousers and a white blouse, fingers pressed to her lips and eyes rounded in surprise? He'd thought about her constantly since the notice of the meeting arrived like a talisman at his home in Colorado. When he'd read her explanation of the restoration she was heading in Rata Cove, and seen her flowing signature at the bottom of the glossy announcement, he'd remembered her big heart, genuine smile, and generous spirit, and knew she was the answer. But it was the face of the eighteen-year-old girl he'd known that filled his mind then, not this confident, poised woman. The chestnut curls she'd worn wild and free as a teenager were now pulled away in a high ponytail, her blue eyes wide. "Cy, it's good to see you."

Memories of summers spent with her flooded him as he settled on the hard wooden bench. The scent of Coppertone sunscreen. The endless ball games on scorching sand, snorkeling in the warm, clear water of the cove. One day stuck hard in his mind. The one and only time he and Ellie had made love. That day, and the life-changing consequences of their actions, seared into his memory.

Realizing Ellie and everyone in the hall was now staring at him, he pulled his thoughts to the present. "I hear some changes are happening here."

"Yes." Ellie cleared her throat before tapping notes on the lectern. Tortoiseshell reading glasses sat on her nose and made her look as confident and in control as she sounded. And she rocked the sexy librarian look that was doing strange things to his chest. "You've heard about the restoration project?" She smiled, and the warmth on her face was a tonic to his jet-lagged brain.

"I'd love to hear more."

She pushed a lock of hair from her face. "As you've read, the council's employed me to lead a restoration project on some of the buildings near the beach. The hall, the old library, the boardwalk in particular, and some of the holiday homes. I'm looking for community input before I finalize my plans." She paused and hooked him with her gaze. "I don't recall seeing you at any of the initial meetings." She glanced down at her notes, then slowly back up at him, and his chest constricted for the time he'd lost with her and the strangers they'd become. "I don't have a submission from you, do I?"

"No, I . . . ah . . . I thought I'd be more help by being here." He hadn't been to Rata Cove, this tiny coastal New Zealand town in nearly a decade, didn't have a right to be part of this, and he wouldn't have returned if he didn't have to ask the biggest favor of his life. "So, where do things stand?"

Ellie glanced at her watch. "This meeting's run its course, Cy. We've been discussing my restoration plans for close to an hour and we need to move out for the New Year's pageant practice."

"I've just arrived in the cove." Weariness filtered into his voice as he dug a hand through his hair. "But I'll take you up on the offer to answer my questions at your cottage."

Ellie nodded, then after a little more general discussion, closed the meeting and people ambled from the hall into the brilliant sunshine. He moved against the flow to reach her, greeting people he hadn't seen in years. One of his old surfing mates said hi and introduced Cy to his kids, and Tom from the store slapped him on the back and told him to stop by for a chat and the town's famous meat pie. As he drew closer to the front, he caught the end of conversations.

"We're so lucky to have you do this, Ellison," an elderly man said as he tipped his cap to her. "Things have been looking tired and run-down for years. We've all got faith you'll turn things around and people will holiday in the cove again."

"Thanks so much, Max." She touched the old guy's wrinkled hand. "It's great to have everyone's support."

"Thank you, Ellie. Harry and I can't wait to see the changes you're going to make," Betty Browning said as she shooed small children in front of her. "It seems like yesterday you were performing in the New Year's pageant on this stage, and now look at you. All grown up and important and living in different counties around the world."

Ellie's eyes sparkled as she smiled.

When the last of the people had moved away, Cy stepped forward and the air between them stilled.

"Ellie, it's great to see you."

Her back straightened, and she clasped her hands in front. Of course she wouldn't lean in for a kiss on the cheek. He hadn't spoken to her since the day after she'd said she loved him, and he'd turned his back on her and left the cove for good. And he couldn't blame her one bit.

Her lips rolled together, and her penetrating gaze hooked his. "To be honest, I was a bit stunned when you walked through the door. I thought you lived in the States. That's where I sent the homeowner's meeting notice. No one's been at your holiday house for ages."

Lines of tension played around her eyes. Her questioning gaze drifted across his face. In eight years, she'd become even more radiant, more animated than he remembered. The beauty of a girl had bloomed into a gorgeous woman, but frost hung in her tone.

"It's been a long time." The words of a detached stranger had come out his mouth before he could stop them. He'd never been unsettled talking to beautiful women before, but this was Ellie, someone who, despite his best intentions, he'd hurt badly. "So, you're an architect, right? Specializing in coastal properties?"

"Yes." A smile played at her lips as she picked up her suit jacket from the back of a chair and rested it over her arm. She shook her head and a soft chestnut ringlet escaped from her ponytail. "I just can't believe you're here. I've caught up with your mum and sister over the years, and they've missed seeing you back in the cove for holidays."

She'd changed so much and yet hardly at all. But there was something new, a secret, womanly power he could sense growing the longer he stood there. Of course, he'd thought about her through the years, regretting they'd lost touch, wishing he'd done more to build a bridge after all they'd been through. Looking at her now, though, no one would know the dark places she'd come from. Seeing this confidence in her confirmed she was the perfect choice for his custody plan, and if that all went well, who knew how their relationship might develop?

He slung hands in the pockets of his jeans. "I can't believe I waited so long to come back. Knowing how much you've always loved the cove, I understand how important this restoration must be for you, Ellie. I'd like to know more."

She picked up the small leather satchel and held it in front of her. "I'm really sorry, but I don't have time to talk about this now. My sister Fleur and her son Louis are here for Christmas, but let's catch up sometime."

Catch up sometime? He shouldn't have expected her to be more welcoming, but it was a slug to the heart. He rocked back on his heels. "Fleur and Louis? Wow, he was just a baby when I last saw him."

She nodded and glanced toward the door.

"No problem, we can catch up later," he said. "Do you live here now?"

She laughed. "I wish. Work takes me around the country and the world, but I try to get back to the cove for the holidays. I'll be spending the next few months managing the start of this restoration, then I'm off to an island in Greece for the rest of the year." She grinned and lifted an eyebrow. "It's a tough job but someone's gotta do it." She flicked her wrist and looked at a bright blue watch. "Sorry, but I need to open the cottage for Fleur. You can ask questions about the project while walking there if you like."

He nodded and followed her out into the sunshine.

***

When Ellie pushed her way out into the December afternoon, Cy fell into step beside her. His warm citrus scent kicked up her heartbeat.

"Want me to carry that?" He nodded at her briefcase. "It looks impressively heavy."

She still couldn't believe he was here. The shock of seeing him again lay like a piece of cold stone in her gut. Not that he'd ever know. "I'm fine, thanks."

He looked so different. What had once been a mess of curls kissed golden by hours in the surf, was now the salon cut of a city dweller, glossy and neat? Where multicolored board shorts would've hung low on slim hips, tan chinos contrasted with a black T-shirt.

For so many years she'd imagined this moment, seeing his dazzling smile again, the confident way he walked into a room, but in her dreams it was never like this. Never with him standing like a stranger, asking her about a business project, and she couldn't think of one intelligent thing to say.

She hadn't counted on him being part of the project closest to her heart, though, and she'd have to find a way to deal with it. The longer she spent in Cy Hathaway's company, the quicker she'd fall under his spell—it had happened a hundred times before—but not this time. When she'd told him she loved him all those years ago, he'd turned tail and run, and she'd never put herself in that vulnerable, devastated position again.

"How long are you back?" She kept her attention forward, following the shade from the red-and-green *pōhutukawa* trees nodding over the sand. Cicadas played a symphony in the background, and seagulls hovered in an endless blue sky.

"A couple weeks. There's…" He cleared his throat. "I

need to deal with some things." As he turned to her, his tone shifted. "I think what you're doing here is amazing."

Slowing her steps, she squeezed the handle of her satchel. "Thanks. It's great that the council agreed to fund the restoration. I was really pleased to be asked to oversee it. There's not a lot of time and spare cash for the upkeep of towns like this. I approached the council last year and offered my services and they agreed to let me renovate."

He turned and stared hard at her, his blue eyes shining and her heart did a loop. "You mean, you're doing this for nothing? That must be tough."

She lifted a shoulder and looked him in the eye. "I love this place. It has memories that would've been lost if something wasn't done. It was a no-brainer. My project in Greece should help pay the bills. As long as I get this finished in time."

"They're lucky to have you. My sister tells me you're an expert in your field."

A fizz shot up her spine and she stepped back. He'd been talking to his sister about her? "I love this place too much to let it die."

He scuffed a boot through talc-like sand. "As soon as your letter arrived, I knew I had to come back."

She'd never contacted him after he left, knew that what lay between them was too overpowering to be repaired. "I sent letters to all the homeowners, of course. Not just you."

He nodded, and she continued. "I was surprised you were listed as the owner. Did you buy your parents and sister out?"

Moving slightly, he bunched hands deep in his pockets and the fabric of his shirt pulled tight across his broad, muscled shoulders. "Mum and Kelly don't come here anymore. After Dad finally left, they found the maintenance difficult."

She hid her surprise. His father had left his mother? Cy had been so hurt by his father's affairs, the drama of his parents' relationship when they were teenagers. "How often do you get back to New Zealand from the States?"

"Not much." He looked out to sea, and a muscle flexed at his jaw. That he was even more handsome than he'd been as a teenager seemed impossible, but it was true. His eyes seemed bluer. His cheekbones more pronounced, lips fuller. "I own a chain of surf stores across the States, so I travel a lot. One of my competitors has been looking to buy me out, but I've worked hard to build the business, and I enjoy the challenge of running stores in different states."

He hadn't been back in the few summers Ellie had been here recently. She knew because she'd lost count of the times she'd stood outside his house in a swimsuit and bare feet, daydreaming about what it would be like if they still spent warm days here together. With his family, her sister Fleur, and nephew Louis...and maybe a couple of kids of their own.

She shook her head to remove the crazy little fantasy that sprung itself on her when she least expected it. Years ago they'd made love one tangled, passionate time, and then he'd left and never returned. She was the girl whose grief he'd made his own. He was the boy who still shared a brutal secret. She flicked a piece of hair from her face. "So, if you're here for Christmas, I guess you'll have family coming. I haven't seen your mother or Kelly in years. I'd love to spend time with them."

He picked up a shell and threw it out to sea. "They won't be making it this year."

Something tugged inside her. Cy had come all this way

and wouldn't be spending Christmas with his family? Something wasn't right.

Share it with us, she almost said. *Come and have an orphans' Christmas with Fleur and me and Louis while my parents riverboat down the Danube, or whichever way they'd planned to avoid Christmas at the cove for another year.* But the words jammed in her mouth. Cy seemed preoccupied, closed even, and she wasn't sure how he'd respond.

His voice was hollow. "It'll just be the two of us for Christmas."

"The two of you?"

"Me and my son, Jonty."

"Your son." The beat of her heart almost hijacked more words. "How old is he?"

A dark shadow crawled across his features. She knew the answer. The grim set of his face gave it away.

"He's six."

Her blood turned to ice as the familiar vision of her brother's six-year-old, lifeless body being pulled from the surf stamped for the millionth time in her mind. Her heart thudded, small and cramped in her throat. She set up the barriers as she'd always done, but the pain broke through.

Breathe.

"Ellie, I—"

He turned to her and she swung her attention to the sand to avoid his tortured stare. The day that changed so many lives. They'd been kissing on a yacht when they should've been watching William. He'd know the chill dancing across her skin, the crater widening in her chest.

Her body quaked, and he stepped closer before seeming to think better of it and kept on talking. "My son's never been here. Katie Newport's looking after him at the moment." He shook his head as they drew up in front of his family's holiday home. Surrounded by bleached logs and waist-high seagrass, it seemed to snooze on the sand. "I can't believe she's sixteen."

"I know, it's scary, right? The way time passes."

"Jonty's finding everything strange." He scraped a hand across his jaw. "Being somewhere so new without his own things around him, it's tough."

"So he's never been to New Zealand at Christmas?"

"He's only been to Auckland once when he was two. But that wasn't with me. He's never been to the beach."

She couldn't help the surprise flitter across her face. "You own surf stores and he's never been to the beach?"

"We live in Colorado, that's—" He shifted his eyes away. "We *have* to live in Colorado."

The sun's rays through the trees freckled on his skin as he crossed his arms.

"Is that where his mother lives?"

An indefinable cloud cast across Cy's features, and she could've kicked herself for her question.

You hardly know him anymore. She swallowed. *If you ever did.* "I'm sorry." She waved her hand in apology. "I have no right asking."

"You don't have children, do you?"

She squeezed the handle of the briefcase tighter. "No, I don't. My career's taking off and I'm doing projects all over the world. That's my passion. My love." Movement out the corner of her eye caused her to turn, and from Cy's house came Katie Newport and a small boy with tousled, corn-colored hair. The image of his dad.

"Bringing families back to this place is so important." He looked at his son. "I want Jonty to have the same holidays I did growing up here. The outdoors, the sense of community, the innocence." He threw her a heart-stopping smile, and her skin tingled. "I might live in the States, but I want to know what's going on here. Sorry I missed all the important information at the meeting. Could we meet up to talk later?"

She bit her lip as she watched Katie encouraging the little boy to come forward. Each time the girl tried to touch him, he wrenched his body away and stood staring at them, a brightly colored scarf wound like a bandage around his hand.

Cy walked toward him but stopped a few feet away and crouched, his voice holding a tenderness that misted her vision. "Hey, bud. I bet you had fun with Katie."

The boy didn't reply, but kept staring past his father to Ellie as Cy spoke quietly. "Why don't we go up to the house and have a snack, eh?"

Still, the boy stood rigid and silent.

"I have to get to New Year's pageant practice, Mr. Hathaway," Katie said.

"Sure, Katie. Thanks for looking after Jonty." He paused and tension wrapped around his words. "Was everything all right?"

The pretty girl smiled, but concern creased her flawless forehead. "He didn't want to do anything other than sit on the bed with his scarf. I tried to get him to build a sandcastle but he wouldn't."

"Don't worry. I shouldn't have left him." His voice was light, but the depth of concern on Cy's face hit Ellie like a blunt instrument. "You go," he said to Katie. "And thanks."

"I'll see you later, Jonty. 'Bye, Ellie." Katie shot them both a grin and jogged down the beach.

"Hi there," Ellie chirped as she crouched down. The poor little boy seemed scared stiff, or cripplingly shy. "Your daddy tells me your name's Jonty," she said brightly. "It's nice to meet you, Jonty. What do you think Santa Claus might bring you next week? I'm really hoping he brings me a new boogie board."

Still the little boy stood motionless, staring at her with liquid blue eyes.

Cy turned to her, his face etched with grief. "Ellie, Jonty has selective mutism. He doesn't speak."

*You can preorder **Desperate Measures** ~ Ellie's story here.*

FANCY A FREE NOVELLA?

Throughout my career, my readers have been such a key part of my writing life, and I love to keep them up to date with what I'm doing. I occasionally send out newsletters with details on new releases and extra special offers for both my books and others like mine. I promise I won't bombard you!

If you sign up to the mailing list, the first thing I'll send you is a **FREE** novella, *Waiting on Forever*, is Alex and Mara's story, and the prequel to my ***Tall, Dark and Driven*** series.

Waiting on Forever

One last task to complete, then Alex Panos can fulfill a heart-breaking promise. That is, if he can get past cute and quirky Mara Hemmingway.

On her own since she was sixteen, Mara won't be taken advantage of again—especially not by brooding and troubled Alex. Instead, she'll play him at his own game.

When their powerful attraction threatens to get in the way of

APPLY TO JOIN BARBARA'S REVIEW TEAM!

If you really enjoyed *Bad Reputations* and fancy reading a lot more about the crazy, lovable people of Brentwood Bay and beyond, apply to join Barbara's review team!

Barbara is now taking applications to join her Advanced Review team. If you're selected, you'll get all of Barbara's releases free, up to a month before release!

Fill out an application **here** or email: barb@barbaradeleo.com

ABOUT BARBARA

Multi award winning author, Barbara DeLeo's first book, co-written with her best friend, was a story about beauty queens in space. She was eleven, and the sole, handwritten copy was lost years ago much to everyone's relief. It's some small miracle that she kept the faith and now lives her dream of writing sparkling contemporary romance with unforgettable characters.

Degrees in English and Psychology, and a career as an English teacher, fueled Barbara's passion for people and stories, and a number of years living in Europe —primarily in Athens, Greece—gave her a love for romantic settings.

Discovering she was having her second set of twins in two years, Barbara knew she must be paying penance for being disorganized in a previous life and now uses every spare second to create her stories.With every word she writes, Barbara is sharing her belief in the transformational power of loving relationships.

Married to her winemaker hero for twenty two years, Barbara's happiest when she's getting to know her latest cast of characters. She still loves telling stories about finding love in all the wrong places, but now without a beauty queen or spaceship in sight.

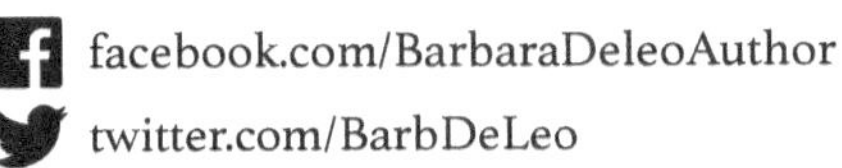

facebook.com/BarbaraDeleoAuthor

twitter.com/BarbDeLeo

ALSO BY BARBARA DELEO

The Breaking Through series

All books can be read as stand alone.

Desperate Measures—Book 2 ~Ellie's story ~ available on Amazon here .

____

The Tall, Dark and Driven series

All books can be read as stand alone

Waiting on Forever—prequel novella ~ **Alex's story** ~ available **FREE** here or email barb@barbaradeleo.com

Ask for Barbara DeLeo's books at your local bookstore, library, or on the Amazon links below.

Making the Love List —Book 1~Yasmin's story ~ available on Amazon here.

Winning the Wedding War—Book 2~Nick's story ~ available on Amazon here.

Reining in the Rebel —Book 3 ~Ari's story~ available on Amazon here.

A Home for Summer—Book 4 ~ Costa's story ~ available on Amazon here.

A Marriage for Show—Book 5 ~ Christo's story ~ available on Amazon here.

A Family for Good—Book 6 ~ Markus's story ~ available on Amazon here.